MONSTROUS HEAT

DYNOSAUROS
BOOK 1

JOELY SUE BURKHART

Copyright © 2022 Joely Sue Burkhart

Cover Art by Moonstruck Cover Design & Photography
www.MoonstruckCoverDesign.com

All rights reserved. No part of this book may be reproduced, scanned, or distributed in print or electronic form without the express, written permission of the author.

This is a work of fiction. Names, characters, places and incidents are the product of the author's imagination and any resemblance to any organization, event, or person, living or dead, is purely coincidental.

Adult Reading Material

❀ Created with Vellum

MONSTROUS HEAT
DYNOSAUROS BOOK 1

I'm lost in the jungle, and something is stalking me.

Discovering a Mayan ruin in the Guatemalan jungle should have catapulted my archeology career, but I'm lost hours from camp. Worse, something is stalking me. It's not a jaguar. It's bigger than anything I've ever seen before and wicked fast. I can't outrun it. I don't have any weapons.

When it catches me…

I can't help but think I've fallen back through time to the Jurassic Period, because the creature looks like a T-rex and raptor had a very vicious baby. It's hungry, too. Very hungry. Though it doesn't hurt me. Yet.

Then a naked man comes to my rescue. Not sus at all.

Kroktl says his squad is on a top-secret mission to Earth, and his outrageous physique certainly fits the part of a lab-created super-soldier alien. Who coincidentally smells exactly like the dino-predator that chased me.

He claims that I can help him through the heat. By the burning way he looks at me, he doesn't mean air temperature. In fact, I suspect that I'm next on the menu. After he plays with his food. He's even calling his squad to come see what he caught.

I don't think I'm getting out of the jungle alive.

For my Beloved Sis.

*Thank you to Sherri Meyer
for all your help and late night edits!*

1

NATALIE

I'm not going to let some jerkoff steal my own fucking discovery. Fuming, I stared at my mentor while resisting the urge to rip him a new asshole. That wouldn't look very good on my academic record, now would it?

"I knew you were the perfect assistant to bring along," Dr. James Snyder gushed. "I'm sure to get a terrific write up in the *Quarterly Archeology Review*. Great job, sweetie."

I'm not your sweetie, dickwad. I ground my teeth and mentally counted to ten. I had to be professional, even if I'd like nothing better than to kick him in the nuts. He controlled my fate, from how excruciating my thesis defense would be to whether the university decided to offer me an assistant professor position. "You *are* going to credit me in the article."

His eyes widened at my firm and assertive voice, pretending to be wounded that I'd even suspect him of stealing credit for finding the ruin. "Of course, sweetie. You're my assistant after all."

Assistant my ass.

I'd been fascinated by a fifty-year-old picture of a crumbling stone doorway that had been carved to resemble a massive mouth complete with fangs. The site had never been fully explored, and after the original archaeologist died, the ruins had been lost once more. I'd meticulously studied the man's journals and articles to track the path he'd taken from the Yucatan Peninsula, through the jungles of Guatemala and Belize and eventually to the coast in Honduras where he'd departed for the UK. When I'd pinpointed a possible area in the Maya Biosphere Reserve in Guatemala, Dr. Snyder had agreed to take me along as his assistant, a position coveted by all the grad students and associate professors trying to elevate their game.

He might be a misogynist prick, but Snyder's charming good looks and clout in archeology circles forced his female students to overlook his many faults. He fancied himself a modern-day Indiana Jones and even wore a ridiculous hat like the famous movie archeologist. Unlike the movie, archeology wasn't a booming, lucrative industry with tons of potential. Positions were few, far between, and quite honestly, mostly given to men. A fact which burned like acid in the pit of my stomach.

I did literally *all* the legwork for this find. I tramped foot by foot through miles of jungle to investigate every suspicious mound, hill, or pile of rock that had been swallowed up centuries ago.

While he sat back at camp taking selfies and preening for his podcast channel.

At last, I'd pinpointed a possible location for the city. The jungle had done its best to swallow every clue, but I'd finally found a man-made stone wall that potentially marked the city's boundary.

"Keep me posted on how many buildings are still intact," Dr. Snyder said. "Plot out everything you can identify on the map as a possible site and enlist Tomas and Jairo to help."

"What about you?" I blurted out as he turned away.

He turned back with a quizzical arch to his brow. With the sun blazing behind him, his golden hair cast a nimbus about his face. "Me? I'll be back at Paso Caballos. Someone has to wine and dine the right people to make sure our dig can continue as planned." He slapped at a buzzing insect and grimaced at the smear on his pristine white shirt. "I can't endure more than a day or two of camping. I'm allergic, you know."

So he'd only stayed in the jungle long enough to ensure that I actually found something—that he could claim for himself. While he abandoned me to do all the work, living it up at the posh hotel catering to tourists. Perfect.

"I'll let you write up the article and we'll see how it goes. It'll be good practice for you if you're hoping to gain a permanent spot at the university."

Of course, he had to get a dig in, making sure to remind me exactly how "helpful" he could be. But the fuck if I was going to do all the physical work and write everything up, so all he had to do was slap his John Hancock on my fucking research. "Now listen here—"

I clamped my mouth shut when the only other graduate student along on the dig, Holly Price, joined us. Her figure made men drool, her long, black hair was fantastic, and she possessed a terrific fashion sense.

"Ah, there you are, my dear." Dr. Snyder gave me a careless wave and tucked Holly's hand beneath his arm. He probably thought it was a gentlemanly, old-fashioned thing to do, but Holly shot me a look of pure horror.

If he'd brought me along to do the physical labor…and he was taking Holly back to the hotel…

"Can't Holly stay?" I called after them. "I could sure use the help."

"I need Miss Price's assistance in town. I'm sure you can manage quite well on your own."

Holly mouthed, *"help me!"* but I could only shrug miserably. What could I do? We were both unfortunately at Dr. Snyder's mercy. We could hike back to the road and try to flag down a local, but he'd paid for the entire trip out of his stipend. He had our tickets. Holly's gorgeous wardrobe suggested money and lots of it, but she'd admitted over a beer at the airport that she was broke too. We'd both spent entirely too many years in college learning about our outdated passion for lost worlds, though in Holly's case, her fascination revolved around how ancient cultures used the mostly now-extinct plants in their daily lives.

In a matter of seconds, they were both gone. Towering kapoc trees and thick underbrush swallowed the faint trail, marked only by machete marks through the dense reserve. It'd take them at least two or three hours to hike back to the dirt road pitted with craters and ruts the size of canyons.

I turned in a slow circle, looking around the jungle. The heavy, humid air pressed inward, trying to suffocate me. Miles away from civilization and on my own, except for two local guides that Dr. Snyder had hired. They seemed nice enough, but I couldn't believe that he'd left a female student alone in the middle of the jungle, so he could try to get lucky with the prettier student he'd brought along.

Some days I hate men. I really do.

Okay, most days. Or maybe the only men I'd ever met were self-absorbed pricks.

Sighing, I pulled out my map. Scanning the trees on all sides, I tried to identify any possible buildings or ruins. Numerous mounds might be piles of stones—or merely tangled vines and snake dens.

I turned to the guides. My Spanish was passable, but thankfully they understood English well enough too. "We're going to carefully comb these trees, inch by inch. If you see a single rock, we'll mark it on the map. Even a fallen-down cornerstone might have inscriptions that will tell us the name of this city."

"I don't know the name of the city," Tomas said gravely, tipping his head toward the stone carvings. "But I know this."

"You do? What is it?"

He touched the stone fangs carved in the wall and then shared a dark look with the other man. "Monster."

2

NATALIE

Wincing, I slowly climbed to my feet. My knees throbbed and my toes burned with pins and needles. How long had I been kneeling on the ground? The pile of what looked like a thousand years of dead leaves had ended up revealing a magnificent stelae, fallen but intact. It weighed a ton, so I couldn't examine the back of it, but it looked as though every inch of stone had been painstakingly carved with glyphs. I could pick out a few here and there, but I was far from an expert. Each section would be carefully photographed and sent to the best cryptologist the university could find.

The name of this once-great city would be on that stelae. Or at least the founding king's name. All in all, we'd managed to find twenty structures or man-made stonework scattered through the jungle. Nothing as grand as Tikal or the famous pyramid at Chich'en Itza, but still an important and yet undocumented find.

Turning around, I looked for Tomas but didn't see the guides anywhere. "Hello?"

I listened, straining to hear anything. The bird calls and

monkey screeches had been loud all day, but now I couldn't hear a thing but the constant drone of insects. "Tomas? Where are you?"

I retraced my steps toward the stone wall that had once marked the entrance to the city. It took me thirty minutes—which surprised me. Surely I hadn't wandered that far out into the jungle. We'd split up after lunch, hoping to cover more ground. I tried to remember what time that'd been. Late. Two? Three? It was nearly dark now.

"Hello? Anyone here?"

At the wall lined with stone teeth, I found a piece of paper stuck beneath a rock.

Emergency. My wife is expecting our first baby. Be back as soon as we can. Sorry.

Greeeeeaaaaat. So not only had the professor abandoned me, but also my guides as well.

My stomach pitched queasily but I made myself take a deep breath. Think. I had to be smart about this.

Hydrate. I hadn't taken a single drink for hours.

I pulled a water bottle from my pack and took a long drink, making a mental list of options. I could wait here for the guides. They knew exactly where I was and would surely come back for me as soon as they could. Probably tomorrow. I'd be alone at night in the jungle with no shelter, no food, and no protection from the animals.

Or I could hike down to the camp. It'd taken us two hours to discover the stone wall this morning, but we'd been painstakingly combing every suspicious-looking pile of leaves and earth, hoping to find a man-made structure. I could probably make it back to camp in under an hour. All I had to do was follow the trail.

It wouldn't be easy in the dark. We'd traveled up and down through some pretty rough ground and the undergrowth had been nearly impenetrable in places. But that would be to my advantage.

All I need to do is follow the hacked-up bushes back to camp. Easy peasy.

I folded the map up neatly and tucked it into my backpack. On the off chance that Dr. Snyder had second thoughts, I checked my phone, but found no flowery messages inviting me to come down to the hotel. I still had a good charge, since I hadn't used it all day. I even had a bar if I held it over my head.

For the barest moment, I considered calling him for help, but quickly rejected it. Would he really skip out on his expensive business meetings and hot date with Holly to come rescue the stupid assistant he'd duped into doing all his research?

Of course not.

Besides, the last thing I wanted to do was call him and beg for help.

Follow the trail, Nat. That's all you have to do.

3

NATALIE

One moment I could see the ground in front of me, and the next, I couldn't see my hand in front of my face. Luckily, I'd come prepared. I had not one, but two spare sets of flashlight batteries in my backpack. I refused to be stuck with dead batteries at the worst possible moment. Along with an extra battery for my phone, in case I couldn't make it back to camp as planned, bug spray, a small roll of bandages, a couple of bags of trail mix, and a chocolate bar. Okay, three candy bars. You never knew when you were going to have a chocolate emergency.

After I fell the first time and bloodied my knee, I was thankful for the bandage. After the second, it was definitely time for chocolate.

"Way to go, Nat," I muttered under my breath, swiping away tears. "You just had to study archeology. Look where eight years of college has gotten you. Stranded in the middle of a Guatemalan jungle."

At least it was way cooler than the daytime. Maybe too cool. Sweat chilled on my skin. I'd definitely be grateful for my cozy sleeping bag and tent. A change of clothes and hot cup of tea, and I'd feel way better. *I just have to get there.*

Grimly, I climbed to my feet and trudged ahead, scanning the ground constantly for pitfalls. The jungle howled and screeched like a living thing all on its own, adding to my jangled nerves. I'd never heard so many animal calls before. I tried to imagine what kind of animal would make those sounds but decided that I had too good of an imagination for that game.

A particularly loud screech made me jerk to a halt. *What the hell...?*

The jungle silenced around me, an eerie dearth of sound after the cacophony. A jaguar? It'd certainly sounded like a predator.

My hands started shaking. My legs tensed, prepared to run. Run where? I had no idea how far camp might be, and I didn't have any hope of outrunning a big cat. It'd probably just lie in wait on a limb and jump on me as soon as I ran right underneath it.

I jerked the flashlight up and scanned the branches overhead. No big glowing eyes reflected back. As quietly as possible, I crept down the path. At least it was a little wider now, a real dirt path rather than a few hacked-up branches to mark the way. But maybe that was a bad thing. Maybe this was a game trail and that big cat was hungry. Of course, it'd hang out near a game trail or a water source. *Shit.*

Everything in me screamed to run, but my brain held on to reason against the panic flailing inside me. Running was bad. I didn't know what was out there. I'd already fallen twice. If I got seriously injured while the guides were gone, I'd probably die waiting on them to find me.

Silence weighed heavier, a complete absence of sound that made my heart pound.

Something was out there. Following me. Or at least

watching me. Something that scared all the other animals into silence.

The metallic screech roared through the night again, so loud and close that I couldn't suppress the terrified squeak that escaped my mouth. I clamped my hands over my ears, nearly fumbling the flashlight. Crouched against a thick tree, I flicked off the light and pressed against the rough bark, trying to disappear. Or at least be as small as possible.

Predators hunt by smell so it won't matter. It'll still find me.

I wanted to smack that know-it-all voice inside my head.

Leaves rustled. A low whuffing snort. Maybe it was a wild boar. Was that better than a jaguar?

Something moved in the shadows. A sharp click, like the tap of a hammer. *Tap, tap.*

What the fuck is that? I strained to see anything that would give me a clue. Stay? Run? Scream?

Though running away really wasn't my style.

I straightened from a crouch. My pulse thundered in my ears as I stepped out onto the trail. I squared my shoulders and lifted my head high. Better to appear as big as possible.

The *tap, tap, tap* came again, drawing my gaze to a thick, dark shadow about ten feet down the trail. Between me and camp. Of fucking course. Huge, too, and way too tall and wide to be a jaguar. Nothing moved, and it was too dark to be sure.

Maybe it's a bushy tree. I'll have a good laugh at myself for being so scared.

Firming my voice into the loudest, meanest *I'm-only-the-professor's-teaching-assistant-but-sit-your-ass-down-anyway* tone I could muster, I yelled, "Get! Get out of here! Leave me alone!"

The low whuffing came again, a deep, rough *huff, huff, huff.* Almost like a laugh. A dare.

Tipping my chin up, I marched down the path, refusing

to look at the mysterious dark shape. It had to be a trick. An illusion that my terrified mind had created. No animal was that tall. The dark blob towered over my head. It had to be a tree all twisted up in vines. Or maybe some long-lost stelae, swallowed by the jungle. That was far more likely than a... giraffe.

Tap, tap, tap.

Despite my bravado, I jerked to a halt. So close. Stiffly, I held myself very still, straining all my senses. No other sound, but that smell. What was it? A kind of musky scent, not completely unpleasant but foreign and strange. It didn't belong. Hairs prickled on my nape and goosebumps raced down my arms. I hadn't smelled anything like that all day. A bear? No, it didn't smell like fur. Besides, there were certainly no bears—or giraffes for that matter—in Guatemala.

A slight movement caught my eye. Something glittered on the ground, catching the fragile moonlight filtering down through the canopy. Black and sparkly, almost like a crystal. The Maya had used obsidian for some of their blades and ornaments. Despite my fear, my heart leaped with excitement. That would be an extremely interesting find, especially if it was an intact blade. It was big enough to be a knife, at least six inches long.

I started to bend down to pick it up. Then I noticed another one. Just like it. No, three.

And then the longest one moved.

Tap, tap, tap.

Claws. Black. Long. Certainly big enough to gut me like a fish. Or lop off my head with one powerful swipe.

I bolted. Blind with terror, I ran, pushing through the trees. Off the path. It didn't matter where. I had to get away.

The jungle seemed to come alive, fighting to trap me for whatever that... *thing*... was. No way in hell that claw belonged on anything that was indigenous to Guatemala. Branches clutched at me, ripping at my hair and clothes. Roots snagged at my feet. I tripped and caught myself on my hands, scrambling like a crab over a huge fallen tree. I fell into the hollow behind it. Probably the hole left from its roots. I huddled there, hoping maybe I'd lost the…

Tomas's word played back to me. The symbol on the stone wall.

Monster.

4

KROKTL

At least she didn't scream. That would have brought out the predator's urges stronger than ever.

Crouched on a crumbling tree trunk, I stared at her huddled form and swallowed back the vicious roar sure to send her tearing off into the jungle again. *Mine!*

I'd thought the betrayal that had stranded my squad on this forsaken hunk of rock was the worst possible thing that could happen to me. Until I went into heat on a planet with no compatible females.

Zero.

Thick, musky fluid leaked from my temples, and I reeked like a prime stud in full breeding frenzy. I'd tried to ease the driving urge by finding a human woman, but failed time after time. A dynos didn't want to fuck a human.

I only wanted to eat them.

Until this one.

She smelled *right*. Her alluring perfume filled my nostrils and sent a mating urge blazing through me like a solar flare I'd see from a galaxy away.

She's ripe. Incompatible genetics be damned.

I'd eat her, all right. All night long. I'd spread her thighs wide and feast to my heart's content. And when she screamed…

It'd be pleasure, instead of terror, that flavored her scent.

Though I couldn't deny that the sharp spike of fear smelled divine. I could control myself despite her fear—as long as she didn't run again. I might lose control altogether in the heat of a chase.

Apex predators loved nothing more than the hunt, and no animal existed anywhere in the universe more apex than me.

Her shoulders stiffened, her head rising with alarm. I hadn't made any noise, but she still sensed the impending doom of my presence. How?

Digging into the soft earth, she scrambled up out of the hole, using tangled roots for leverage. I waited until she was back on the jungle floor before I pounced.

Fuck, her skin was so fragile. My claws sliced through her shirt and into her flesh despite my care. Blood flavored her scent, a dangerously intoxicating perfume. She twisted in my grip, screaming and flailing. I tried to soothe her, but the low hiss only made her shriek even louder. Without injuring her more, I managed to flip her over onto her back. I planted one rear paw on her midriff. Ever so carefully, I tightened my grip on her until she felt the prick of claws in her tender belly.

Gasping for breath, she stared up at me. Her eyes were huge dark pools of terror. Littered with leaves and debris, her hair was a tangled mess. She wore a plain T-shirt and khaki shorts, but I'd never seen anything more delicious. Curves galore with the courage to walk down that path and at least try to face me down, not even knowing what I might be capable of. And her scent.

Fuck. Sweet and spicy and so fucking hot.

She'd have to chop off my motherfucking head to make me leave her alone now.

"Please," she whispered, her teeth chattering so badly that I could barely understand her. "Don't eat me alive. Kill me quickly. Then you can do whatever you want."

NATALIE

Why doesn't it kill me already and put me out of my misery?

My brain couldn't comprehend what kind of monster pinned me on the ground. A giant lizard? That walked on two powerful hind haunches? With fucking *claws* and razor-sharp *teeth*? Even if it was some kind of Gila monster on radioactive steroids, it wouldn't be upright like this. It wouldn't look at me with such brutal intelligence. Red eyes gleamed like it'd climbed out of the fiery pits of hell. Long head, huge mouth, loaded with teeth as big as my fingers. A single bite would chomp off my whole hand.

Maybe it was a self-preservation necessity but my analytical mind kicked in. Could some kind of mutated crocodile-lizard live in these deep jungles? I'd read every single book in the university's library on Guatemalan myth, culture, and history before leaving the States. The Maya did have a crocodile or earth-monster god. Maybe that god had been inspired by a living, breathing creature they'd found in the darkest reaches of the jungle.

This monster certainly appeared to have age. It didn't look like a lizard. It looked too… prehistoric.

In fact, it looked like some kind of dinosaur.

Way to go, Nat. You not only discovered a lost Maya city but the last living dinosaur. Maybe you should go to Scotland next and document Nessie.

Holding my gaze with those wickedly-knowing demon eyes, the creature lowered its head toward me.

My stomach pitched. My ribs squeezed like iron bands. I couldn't breathe. *It's going to eat me.*

At the last moment, it turned its head and rubbed its scaly cheek against my chest. At least it wasn't slimy or cold, but strangely warm and smooth, almost like textured leather. Braced for rending pain and tearing teeth, it took my brain a second to catch up. The monster made that low hissing sound again and something wet touched my skin. Ugh.

Shuddering, I pushed its head away. "Gross. Stop torturing me and just eat me already!"

It whuffed out that low, raspy huff that sounded like a chuckle. As if I'd made some kind of dirty joke.

Could it actually be intelligent enough to understand every single thing I said? If so…

"If you're done licking me, then get off me, you son of a bitch."

Still rumbling, it sat back on its haunches and lifted its paw, letting me scramble backwards out from under it. I crab-crawled as far as I dared, a foot, two. Until those red eyes slitted and it bared its teeth in warning. Okay. So maybe it wasn't going to eat me. Yet. But it wasn't ready to let me make a run for camp either.

It—*he*—looked at me with stark possession.

His head tipped to the side as he watched me. Probably

trying to estimate how many meals he'd get out of me. The darkness masked most of the details about his shape. Big. Bad. Teeth. Claws. Scales. That much I already knew.

He leaned back in toward me, and I involuntarily reared back, bracing for attack. Holding my gaze, he stretched out a clawed... hand. Almost. The appendage was shorter than his heavily muscled back legs, and the three toes were smaller, more mobile, but still tipped with claws. These wouldn't behead me with a swipe—but would let him hold me down while he raked me with his back claws. Or gripped me tightly for those vicious teeth to get a good grip in my stomach. Or throat. Or—

I gave myself a mental slap. *Calm down. Fear is bad. He'll smell it.*

The claw glittered like a black diamond. Curved like a blade, it was evidently serrated too. I averted my face, trembling, but he slipped the claw against my throat and ripped. My T-shirt. Not my throat. But it still made me gasp and jerk away, inching my butt in the loamy jungle floor. If he got that rear leg on me again, he'd gut me.

He made a clicking noise, still watching me with those eerie eyes. Like he was trying to tell me something. His intensity made my stomach quiver with dread. Was he trying to decide the tastiest morsel to devour first? Or something... worse? Shivering, I clutched the tattered remnants of my shirt. The dumbest thought popped into my head.

At least it's not my favorite Hard Rock Cafe shirt.

I laughed out loud and winced at how hysterical I sounded. Not me. Getting dumped in the jungle by my mentor hadn't rattled me, just pissed me off. Even finding out my guides had been pulled away for an emergency hadn't made me fall apart. But now, if I wasn't careful, I'd be sobbing in a ball and wishing I had a blankie to pull over my head until the scary monster went away.

He touched my arm with that vicious claw. I jerked away, but he wouldn't stop. Not until I stopped trying to avoid it. When I finally looked up at him, his jaws widened enough that it looked like a smile.

Great. A *joking* ravenous monster.

A man yelled in the distance, and the creature's head jerked up. Nostrils flaring, his head scanned left and right. Despite my fear, I had to admit he was brutally beautiful. A killing machine, claws stretched out, teeth bared. Without his attention locked on me like I was a wounded prey animal, I could admire his beauty. Like I'd admire a jaguar. At a zoo. Behind nice protective glass and ten-foot-tall iron fences. No, twenty. Maybe higher. Those back legs looked like muscled springs that would propel him extremely well if he jumped.

I shifted my weight slightly, trying to get my feet under me. His head whipped around and those baleful eyes burned a warning. He stepped closer and turned to the side, giving me his back. As if he wanted me to fucking *climb* on top of his motherfucking *back*.

Hysterics threatened again. "Oh, hell, no. Are you fucking kidding me?"

Something lashed the leaves. A tail. Prehensile too, because he wrapped it around my waist and tugged me closer. I beat my fist on the heavily scaled muscle. "No! No way! Don't touch me, you fucking mutated Godzilla!"

He hissed again and one of those small hand claws dug into the back waistband of my shorts. Kicking and screaming, I bucked in his grip. I couldn't help it. The thought of climbing on top of this... *thing*, having it touch me so closely —I couldn't. My brain felt like spun crystal, splintering toward the full-blown shatter of a million jagged pieces.

With a distinct sound of disgust, he dumped me back down in the root hole. I fell in a graceless heap, sprawled awkwardly on my back. The creature stared at me, that possessive glint in his eyes making me shudder. I didn't need words to understand exactly what he was telling me. *Stay. I'll be back for what's mine.*

He'd ripped my shirt. To get a good look at my tasty stomach, the better to bite me? Or my breasts?

Come on, Nat. He offered you a ride.

I ground my fist against my lips, trying to stifle the hysterical giggles. *I'm losing my ever-loving mind.*

If he wasn't going to eat me…

The creature stared at me, eyes glowing like bonfires. Those wicked teeth parted, and his tongue swiped out. He barked out a hoarse, low cry, and then whirled to tear off into the jungle. Leaves and branches rained down on me with the fury of his passing.

I had a pretty good idea that rough sound had been a demand that I stay put.

Like hell I will.

I scrambled up the side of the hole and ran in the opposite direction. It might not be toward camp, but at this point, all I cared about was getting as far away as possible before that creature came back.

5

NATALIE

My lungs burned and my legs trembled like Jell-O, but I refused to stop. I'd lost both the flashlight and my backpack somewhere. I didn't even remember slipping free of the pack. Maybe it'd caught on a branch, and I'd just run right out of it in my panic.

My phone. Map. Camera. Even if I could find our camp without the trail, would I be able to find the ruins again?

At this point, I honestly didn't care. I'd run until dawn, find a road, a car, anything to haul my ass out of the jungle as fast as it could go. Then I'd hop on the first plane back to the States. Dr. Snyder could find a new dupe to write his research papers.

Too many years in my most favorite place in the whole world—the library—meant that I had to rest and give my lungs a chance to catch up. I ducked beneath the sweeping limbs of a massive tree and crouched down, trying to gasp and heave as quietly as possible. I couldn't hear a thing over the pounding of my heartbeat. My vision swam and my tongue felt like a wad of cotton. I hadn't eaten since lunch, and now I didn't even have my emergency supplies. Nothing looked familiar. For all I knew, I'd run in completely the wrong direction and had crossed into Mexico.

Something hard and powerful snaked around my neck and jerked me back. Panicked that it might be that revolting tail, I clawed at the restraint.

"Shhh," a man whispered against my ear. "There might be more out there."

I drooped against him, relieved it wasn't the monster. "Who are you?"

"Kroktl. You?"

Uh… What an odd name. "Natalie."

He held me tightly against him. His body heat enveloped me, making me realize exactly how cold I'd been. Tall, broad, and strong, he made the jungle feel a little safer. Despite his weird name.

Until I realized that he didn't have on any clothes. Like not even boxers. And he was *very* happy to see me. I caught myself doing a mental measurement and my face blazed with heat. "Um, why are you naked? In the jungle?"

"I heard a ruckus and came to investigate. I have a cabin not far from here."

A ruckus? Surely I hadn't been *that* noisy.

"You're not in the Biosphere any longer. You crossed into the prime drug-trafficking corridor from Mexico that runs out of Laguna del Tigre National Park. There's armed men and hidden airfields scattered all through this section of forest. You're lucky that I found you first."

I'd heard a man shout before the creature had run off. Hopefully it would be too busy feasting on criminals to chase after me. "Wait. How'd you know I was here for the Biosphere?"

"You're dressed like a tourist. The Biosphere is why tourists come here."

He stood, pulling me up with him. He kept me tucked

under his arm, pressed to his side, and headed off into the jungle.

Wait. Are you just going to head off into the wilderness with a strange naked man with a very weird name?

What alternative did I have?

I could sit here lost in the middle of nowhere and hope the monster didn't come back...

"There's a big lizard-thing after me. Have you seen it before?"

"Lizard?" I couldn't see his face, but I heard the smirk in his voice. "That sounds terrifying."

"It was huge! Bigger than you. It picked me up with its tail and tossed me around like I weighed nothing at all." I laughed self-consciously. Way to remind a potentially hot guy that I'm not exactly a model-sized zero.

"No way in hell a lizard is bigger than me." He tightened his arm around my shoulders. "But I assure you that I could haul you around without breaking a sweat."

I caught myself before I could retort, *"prove it,"* biting my tongue. I didn't know this man. He might be saving me now, but for all I knew, he worked for one of the Mexican cartels and was going to use me as a mule. "It wasn't a normal lizard. It looked like some kind of prehistoric monster."

"Maybe you found Chupacabra."

"I don't think Chupacabra are that big. This thing was Godzilla huge."

"Well, no wonder you were terrified. I'm lucky I found you in one piece." In the dark, I tripped on a root, and he scooped me up against his chest without even breaking stride. "I got you."

"How far is your cabin? You can't carry me too long."

He glanced down at me, the hard planes of his face illuminated by a flash of moonlight. He didn't have any hair. Like none whatsoever. Not even stubble. But his lips. *Guh.* That full, sensual bottom lip just begged to be sucked on. No, I wanted to dig my teeth into that delectable lip and hold on for dear life while he fucked me blind.

The thought stunned me. Literally wiped my brain of all function.

I must have fallen and hit my head. Hard. Or I was going into shock.

He shifted me higher in his arms, and it felt natural to tuck my face against the strong column of his throat. His scent washed over me, a deep, rich musk that I recognized immediately because it was so strange and foreign.

Monster.

Oh fuck. No way.

My heart jolted. I stiffened.

The giant lizard thing had that same distinctive odor. Not bad, exactly, but strong and overwhelming. It made me light-headed and scared spitless at the same time.

He rubbed his cheek against the top of my head and a low soothing rumble rolled from deep within his chest. "Don't be afraid, Natalie. I won't hurt you."

KROKTL

Scent. That's how she'd known I was close.

I'd never known a human to be able to smell so well, but

that was just another reason she was meant for me. I simply had to convince her of that fact before anyone came looking for her. I'd do whatever it took to keep her, but I was afraid the second I put her back down on her own two feet that she'd take off again.

Without setting her down, I shifted her in my arms enough to get the door to my cabin open. I really wanted to drop her on my bed and ensure she got a real good taste of what I was offering before her justifiable doubts and fears could take over, but she squirmed in my arms. With a sigh, I set her down and made myself let go of her completely.

I flipped on the light so she could see. The cabin hadn't been much to speak of when I'd claimed it. Deep in the jungle, secluded from all signs of civilization, it was the perfect hideout. The previous owner had rigged up basic but functional indoor plumbing by piping in water. The kitchen was comprised of a two-burner hot plate, a coffee pot, a mini fridge—mostly filled with mediocre beer—and a tiny section of cabinets. Mostly empty. I didn't cook much. Dyni preferred fresh, hot blood and still-kicking meat.

Fuck. I can't even feed her anything but candy bars and coffee.

She made an odd choking sound that brought my attention back to her in a rush.

Mouth open, she stared at me like she'd die if she looked away. Eyes locked on my cock, she licked her lips, and I almost shot my load then and there.

I'd been painfully erect for weeks, whichever form I took. Aching, sweating, mercilessly driven by hormones to hunt for an elusive female and breed. Hard. A simple hand job only made the need worse. I'd endured heat cycles before but nothing like this one, made so much worse by the distinct lack of compatible females on this worthless planet.

Let alone a fucking *mate*. A true mate I'd kill anything and anyone to keep.

I shifted my hips forward, putting my erection on full display to let her drink her fill. Hopefully she wasn't scared off. I wasn't sure how anatomically different I might be from human males. It'd work. I'd make it work. It'd be so fucking good she'd never even think of another male ever again.

Fuck, she smelled good. Her lush scent drove me mad—but also curiously put the dynos at ease. Urgency still hammered through my veins, but I didn't fear the predator would rip out to attack her. In fact, I was pretty sure the fucking beast would flip over on its back and invite a belly rub as soon as she touched me.

She made another soft sound and dragged her gaze up my chest. Tons of scars from bullet wounds, claw marks, and knives, you name it—over shredded muscle. I'd been bred for warfare. Engineered to be the biggest, baddest soldier of the galaxy.

When she finally met my gaze, her eyes were so soft and dazed that I couldn't stifle a low growl. *Yeah, baby. This is all for you.*

Making myself move slowly so I didn't scare her again, I pulled a chilled bottle of water from the fridge. I handed it to her, making sure our fingers brushed. "Drink it slowly, baby. You're probably dehydrated, and it'll make you sick if you drink too fast."

"I'm not your baby," she said it automatically, as though it was something she'd been forced to say a lot to someone.

Eyes narrowed, I kept my voice even despite the immediate surge of aggression that pumped through my veins. "You can be, if you don't already have a…" I almost said *mate* but managed to change it to, "man back home."

She snorted and rolled her eyes. "I don't have a man waiting for me." Her amusement faded, and she dropped her gaze back down to my chest. I could almost feel her eyes tracing the thick scars across my skin. Better if it was her tongue. "I don't have much right now. Probably not even a job when I get back. If I get back."

I wanted to tell her that she didn't need a job, not if she stayed with me. But this must be important to her, or it wouldn't worry her so. "Why's that?"

"This was my big break. I finally made it onto one of Dr. Snyder's research trips, and I'm on the verge of finishing my thesis. I figured I'd be a shoe-in for the next assistant professor position. At the least, I'd be able to help write up our findings and get my name out there in the right circles. But he's going to take all the credit. I'll be lucky if my name is printed anywhere on the article that he'll make me write. Now, I don't even have that. I lost my camera. The map. I don't have any idea where I am. I don't even have proof that I found the ruins at all to force him to keep my name on the paper."

The tremor in her voice made me step closer to her, though her head jerked up. Her eyes sharpened with alert focus, and she sidled backward.

"I'll find your camera. Where'd you leave it?"

"I don't know. It was in my backpack."

It'd be easy for me to sniff out her trail until I found the backpack. But she didn't know what I am. Not yet. She had suspicions, sure. Especially after smelling my bare skin pressed against her face. "I'll find it."

She gave me a small nod, but I read doubt in her eyes. She wasn't sure about me. About any of this.

"Are you hungry? I can probably find you a chocolate bar. Nuts? No nuts? Caramel?"

She snorted out a laugh that made my cock twitch toward her like a hungry beast on its own. "Nuts, always, but water's good for now."

"I have beer. Or better yet, coffee. I can make a pot. Best damned shit you've ever had, grown and roasted just miles away. I'll be packing out as much of it as I can carry when..." I hesitated, not sure how much to say. I didn't want to give her information overload.

Her lips quirked, her eyes sparkled, and fuck, I wanted to crush that delectable mouth beneath mine and sink balls-deep into her warmth. "What if I said I don't drink coffee?"

I took a step closer, and this time, she didn't retreat. Progress. "Then I'd say I could forgive a woman who wouldn't drink beer, but I'd never trust anyone who wouldn't drink coffee."

"Nectar of the gods?" She murmured, her gaze dropping south again.

Just knowing she was looking—and admiring, if the quickening of her breathing was any indication—made my balls tighten with lust. "I've got another nectar in mind, but yeah, coffee's a close second."

"Kroktl?" Her voice trembled as she stumbled over my name.

I froze, forcing my body into compliance. I rasped out, "Yeah?"

"I don't mean to be rude, but..." She gulped and dragged her gaze back up to mine. "You... Uh... You're not exactly..."

I sighed. "Human."

6

NATALIE

If my eyes got any bigger, I was afraid my brain would just roll out on the floor.

Holy shit.

I was right.

Not human.

Inhuman. What did that mean? Demonic? Alien? But he sounded so... normal.

He talked and joked like a guy I'd just met at a bar. Despite his obscenely huge muscles, inhumanly broad shoulders, not to mention the biggest, thickest dick I'd ever seen in my life, he otherwise seemed normal. Though my first thought had been that kind of size was physically impossible. No man could even think about walking around with such a big dick in his pants. Like how would it even fit?

Though my pussy sure wanted to give it a try.

Despite my raging libido, my rational mind was throwing out red flags everywhere. I had no idea what he was. Not human could mean a lot of things. Even the possibility that I'd run into something like him in the jungle would have seemed impossible before the giant lizard thing had chased me.

And yeah, about that. Just remembering the way it had looked at me. Ripped my shirt. Gripped me with those vicious claws.

If that was him… Somehow…

My teeth chattered and it was all I could do not to break into a dead run for the door.

"I'm not from your planet." Ever so slowly, he lifted his hand toward my face. Huge palm, his forearm corded and veined with strength. I couldn't help but remember the sharp claw tearing my shirt. Even though all he did was gently pluck a leaf out of my hair. "My squad was sent here nearly a year ago on a…" He hesitated, as if trying to decide how much to tell me. "Rescue mission. We were stranded. Someone betrayed us. We've been trying to figure out the best way to get back without violating the ordinances put on us."

He paused, letting me think. "There are more of you? Like actual aliens? What planet are you from? How are you going to get back? What about that lizard thing?"

Laughing softly, he pulled another stray leaf out of my hair. "I'll answer all your questions. I swear. But right now, I need you to understand the danger you're in."

My heart thudded heavily. "You *are* going to eat me."

His eyes narrowed into slits, his fingers tightening in my hair. Not to hurt me—but to hold me close. To keep me from backing away. I could feel the weight and strength in his fingers despite the small touch, and though he didn't pull my hair or force me closer, my heart rate doubled.

"I will never hurt you. I know you don't understand what's going on yet, but know that above everything else, I'll kill anyone and anything that threatens you. Do you understand?"

His scent washed over me as if he'd just doused himself in musky cologne. Dizzy, I swayed, trying to think. I had too many questions. Not human. The creature with glowing red eyes. Not from this planet. Alien.

Disjointed words and phrases that should mean something.

"You feel it too," he whispered against my temple. "The heat."

Such a small word to describe what I was feeling. Heat poured from him, as if I'd opened a pizza oven and hot air blasted me in the face. All the air sucked out of my lungs. His scent burned my eyes and nostrils. Numbing me. Or inflaming me like a drug. Because I caught myself touching him, this stranger, smoothing my palms over the wide expanse of his chest as if it was the most natural thing in the world.

Holy fuck. So much muscle. Hot velvet over granite.

My knees trembled, and I had to focus intently to keep my legs from folding beneath me and dumping me on the floor. I had a feeling that he'd catch me before I could fall on my ass but that was a bad idea. Right?

My nipples rubbed faintly against my bra. Liquid heat pooled in my groin. I tried not to think about his mouth. Biting his lip. Wrapping my fingers around his dick just to feel exactly how big it was. Oh fuck.

I'm in serious trouble.

"I'm trying really hard to give you a choice before it's too late."

His words barely penetrated the haze of need fogging my brain. "Choice?"

"I've been in heat for weeks. The pain—" His voice caught on a soft inhale, almost like someone had stabbed him. "I'm in control. Barely. But if you stay, I'm going to have you, Natalie. I'm going to spread you out beneath me and fuck you until you're hoarse from screaming with pleasure. I won't be able to let you go. Ever. Your scent will be imprinted on my mind. I'll track you down anywhere. Back to your home. Off this planet. Another galaxy. I'll find you. I'll drag you kicking and screaming right back onto my dick until you're filled with cum and you can't smell or feel anything but me. You understand me, baby?"

My eyes fluttered, thoughts bouncing around in my head like random ping pong balls. Red flag. So hot. Lust. Red flag. Red flag! Oh fuck. That big, thick dick filling me up—

He gripped my chin, his fingers digging into my skin hard enough that all the bouncing balls crashed to the floor in silence. He leaned down, holding my gaze. I saw it now. Not human. His eyes burned like the monstrous red eyes of the creature.

"I'm in heat," he repeated, each word a rasp of barely controlled violence. "I want to *breed* you. It's all I can think about. If you don't want no part of me, of this, I understand. But you gotta leave now. Better yet, put a couple of bullets in my skull on your way out. Though that won't stop me once I shift."

A hot one-night stand was one thing. But *breeding*? I'd never planned to have kids. Let alone with an alien soldier creature that I'd just met.

His words should have sloshed over my head like an icy bucket, breaking the haze numbing my brain. But my body still hummed with desire. My fingers roamed over the ridged bumps of his washboard abs. Rationally, I knew it was stupid, dangerous, even, to touch a stranger like this. Let alone consider more.

But I couldn't stop.

My tongue felt like a wad of cotton, making me slur my words. "I can't get pregnant. I'm on birth control. I got the shot before I left the States."

Sweat trickled down his forehead, his breathing more labored. "I don't fucking care about no motherfucking shot. I'm super-charged, primed and loaded, engineered to be indestructible. I'm trying to come clean here, Natalie. One time won't be enough. I'll have you again and again until you beg me to stop. No human-made shot is going to keep me from my goal. You can do anything you want to me, and I'll love every second of it, but if you touch my dick, I'm going to come all over you."

Uh… My brain hiccupped. Why would he say that?

Surely that wasn't my fingers tracing the deep vee of muscle that pointed like an arrow to his cock. Intrigued. Intimidated. I couldn't seem to make up my mind which. I wasn't the kind of woman to ogle or objectify a man, but I couldn't seem to take my gaze off his erection.

Wondering if I could wrap my fingers around it. If it would feel like a human cock—or something as alien and foreign as the dinosaur-thing. If I could even physically take him inside me. He just looked too damned big.

And I couldn't stop looking. Or thinking. Or touching…

Lightly, I touched the tip of my finger to the head of his cock.

His head fell back, his shoulders and neck corded, tendons rising like something was trying to tear out of his body. For a moment, I was terrified his skin would split open and the creature would crawl out. Shuddering, he growled, deep and low and so vicious that my scalp tingled with alarm, even as he shot thick streams of cum onto my stomach.

Warm and thick, soaking through the torn remnants of my shirt. A fresh, hot wave of musk enveloped me. Adrenaline coursed through my veins, sending my heart rate skyrocketing.

Chase. Hunt. Danger.

Though I couldn't move, let alone think about running away. My knees wobbled and I caught his arm to keep my balance.

Breathing hard, he tugged my sticky shirt up. His fingers searingly hot on my stomach, he rubbed his cum into my skin. Marking me. With the thick musky scent.

"Yes," he growled, so raw and feral that I could barely understand him. "I'm going to come on every inch of you. Rub my scent into you until you reek of me. I'm going to mark you. My teeth in your throat. My cock in that tight little pussy. While I make you come so many times you'll beg me to stop. If that don't sound good to you, then tell me now. A loaded gun is taped to the bottom of the counter. Empty all the rounds into me. Aim for my skull. That'll slow me down enough for you to get away."

Involuntarily, I shuddered, shaking my head. "No. I can't. I won't do that to you."

His breath sawed in and out. His shoulders seemed broader, his chest thick and huge, his arms even more massive. As if the creature strained inside him. I still couldn't quite wrap my mind around it, but I knew the thing in the jungle was inside him. Somehow.

The creature hadn't hurt me then.

I had to hope it wouldn't hurt me now.

Because mistake or not, I couldn't resist the curiosity that burned inside me. I wanted to feel that same ferocious strength straining on top of me. Feel that beast hovering so close. Dangerous, yes. But intoxicating.

Dragging my gaze up his body to his face, I caught the red flash in his eyes again. His neck and shoulders corded with strain. Sweat beaded on his brow, his nostrils flaring with each breath. But he waited for me to decide.

That told me more than anything what kind of man he was. Despite his strength and obvious need, despite the monster bulging inside him, he wouldn't hurt me. Even to ease his own pain.

I dug my fingers into his arm, looped my other arm around his neck, and let my knees sag. As I expected, he caught me up against him. Thick, hard muscle and burning skin against me, stealing my breath. I couldn't help but notice his erection was as big as before, unfazed by his release.

His breath was hot against my ear. A beast prowling the jungle in search of prey. "Tell me what you want."

"I want you."

7

NATALIE

He swept me up and tossed me down so quickly that I barely had time to register the mattress beneath me. Something tugged, hard, right over my breastbone, and my bra split in half. The sound of tearing cloth was obnoxiously loud. My hips jerked up, shorts ripping open. Goosebumps raced down my arms. Claws?

Though he felt normal against me, not like scales. Hot skin, muscle, the crushing weight of his body against me. The lighting wasn't that great though I could still see. Massive shoulders blocked the bare bulb dangling from the ceiling. His mouth sealed over mine, wiping every last thought from my mind.

Lips wide open, his tongue slid deep on a possessive stroke inside my mouth like he had to taste me or die. Clutching his shoulders, I gave him my tongue too, shivering as he sucked me deeper. His teeth felt normal. Human. Not jagged monstrous jaws to rip me limb from limb. His tongue swept over mine, his lips inhaling me in wet heat unlike any kiss I'd ever had. Like he was trying to put my whole face in his mouth.

Lifting his head, he swept his tongue over my lips, leaving me tingling and damp. Breathing open mouthed and more than a little shell shocked. Hallucinating, maybe. Because his eyes glittered like rubies, spinning a red cast around the room. Then he was gone from my line of vision.

His hands clamped around my thighs. He jerked me closer to him, bending my knees up. His tongue swirled over my knee, startling me. That was not a place I ever thought about him licking. It didn't feel bad, just weird. Hot. The way he flattened his tongue and swirled over my flesh had me biting back a whimper.

He must have heard that stifled cry. Pushing my knees back toward the mattress, he splayed me wide. I could feel the pant of his breath on my skin. Hear the ragged inhale. I could only imagine what I smelled like after working all day in the humid jungle. It wasn't like we had a five-star shower in camp, either. Mentally, I cringed, my thighs automatically trying to close. I should have—

"Pure torture, baby." He sucked in another deep breath. "I've been dreaming of this since I caught the first tantalizing whiff of you."

He pushed me wider, wedging his shoulders between my thighs so he could rub his entire face against me. Not just his tongue and lips, but his nose. His chin. Coating his face. His tongue flattened wide, scraping up over my flesh from top to bottom. He threw his head back, licking his lips. A deep, guttural sound rumbled the entire bed and then he dived back in between my thighs.

Pleasure coiled through me like a deep, winding river. I'd never had a man explore my pussy so thoroughly. As if he had all the time in the world. As if his own need didn't matter. He wasn't even trying to get me off, because he avoided my clit entirely. He kept rumbling and groaning against me, almost like he was feasting. The vibration of his lips increased the sensation of his tongue flowing over me. He sucked on my flesh, pulling my tender bits into his mouth. I could feel his teeth grazing over me, but he didn't bite.

I strained against his grip, trying to lift my hips. Move his mouth up to where I wanted.

He lifted his head a little, peering up at me with lazy, hungry eyes. Predator eyes. Stalking me again. Taking his time before he set in for the feast.

Taking what he wanted.

A cry escaped my lips. A soft, fragile sound that he evidently loved. His tongue speared me, licking inside as if he couldn't get enough of my taste. I quivered, unable to lie still. I fisted my hands in the sheets, trying not to cry out again, but it was a losing battle. I bit my lip and another moan escaped.

He made another broad pass with his tongue, circling his head to cover as much of my pussy as possible. Reward. For my sounds. I got it now.

I'd never been very loud in the bedroom before. Partly my personality, my nature, but mostly due to my inherent sense of self preservation. Especially against strange men that I didn't know very well.

Like this man with the weird name who had freaky red eyes and made scary sounds.

He wasn't human. Which should have made it even more difficult for me to let down my defenses and trust him. But somehow, it made it easier. He wasn't like any other man I'd ever known. How he could be so huge and strong and terrifying—yet also careful and considerate at the same time. He could have hurt me. Badly.

Yet all he did was pin me down on his bed and lick my pussy until I wanted to sob.

If that was what it'd take to get his mouth on my clit, then

I'd burst his eardrums. I wanted to come, yes, but I wanted to get him inside me. I wanted to feel him on top of me. Not holding me down for more torture.

I dropped the last of my reserves and sank into the overwhelming sensations coursing through me. The formidable strength of his fingers digging into my thighs, pushing me wider. The stroke of his tongue. I swore it was longer and thicker than any tongue had a right to be. My imagination? Or part of his alien abilities? I had no fucking clue but if his tongue felt so incredible, I could only imagine how good his cock would feel.

Deep, raw sounds escaped my throat. Part groan, part plea. More. Hurry. I couldn't seem to find my voice to say the words. But he understood.

His lips closed around my clit, his tongue nudging up against it, holding me like a delicate candy against the roof of his mouth while he sucked.

I climaxed so hard that I was pretty sure that my soul left my body.

My head slammed down, every muscle clenched. I screamed so loudly the drug smugglers were probably all headed straight to our location. I tore at his shoulders, trying to get him to come up my body, but he only sucked harder. His teeth dug in around my clit, a delicious threat. The knowledge that he could bite a hunk out of me even without shifting to the monster with the razor-sharp teeth sent a sharp zing of adrenaline through me.

Which only ratcheted my climax higher.

He pressed a biting kiss to my inner thigh with enough pressure to leave teeth marks. It almost hurt too much—dancing down that fine line between pain and pleasure. He moved up my body, dropping more open-mouthed kisses. A brush of teeth. His tongue wrapped around my breast, hot and wet, rasping over my nipple. Every stroke of his tongue sent another shot of electricity rippling through my nerves all the way back down to my clit.

Another pulse of pleasure rocked through me. A ceaseless wave that rippled up through my body, arching my back. My eyes rolled back in my head. Or maybe I passed out a moment. He loomed over me, a towering mountain of muscle, but he cupped my nape in his palm, his fingers splayed in my hair.

"You still with me?" His voice was ragged and raw with strain. "Natalie?"

Words were beyond me, but I managed to focus on his eyes. Searing red. But I could almost read a pattern in the glow. Circles, lines, maybe rapid letters scrolling across the screen. Like a robot? Or a computer screen maybe. A machine.

Though nothing about him felt mechanical. Only hot, living flesh and bone and muscle flowing against me.

"Natalie?" he repeated. "Last chance. Stop me now. Once I'm inside you…"

Another wave of pleasure crested through me with his words. He wasn't even inside me yet, but I couldn't stop coming. Maybe it was his scent, filling my head and firing my blood like an aphrodisiac, though partly because he was still so concerned about making sure he still had my consent. That I was still okay. Hadn't changed my mind. Even with a giant raging erection hovering at the ready.

One corner of my mouth quirked up and I managed to string words together. "I can touch your dick again…"

"Fuck." He shuddered, his breath hissing out between his teeth. "I'm getting inside you this time."

Gently setting my head back on the pillow, he reared back on his knees between my thighs, lifting my hips so my ass lay against the tops of his legs. Some of the haze cleared as I looked up at him. Measuring exactly how big that dick was up close and personal...

I didn't change my mind—but I couldn't help but tense up. My thighs quivered and trembled. I braced myself, holding my breath against what I feared might hurt. A lot.

He fisted his cock and rubbed the head up and down my slit. He didn't try to get inside me yet. Slow and easy despite the way his breath sawed in and out of his chest, he rubbed his dick against all the wetness he'd generated, stroking my engorged flesh. Reminding me of exactly how good his tongue had felt. How hard I'd come just a few minutes ago.

So slick. He glided back and forth over my pussy with ease. Deep, molten heat spread through my groin. A tiny corner of my mind—that somehow managed to stay rational despite the sensual overload—wondered if he was leaking something on me. A natural lubricant. Pre-cum, maybe? Something that heated and primed me even more than his mouth had done.

My hips twitched up, deepening his stroke. Pushing my groin up against the smooth, steady glide of his dick. Inviting him inside.

A deep, guttural sound rumbled through him. Almost a purr but more... reptilian. It sent chills screeching down my spine, even as my back arched, pushing up against him. Pressure built against my opening. No pain but more than a little intimidating. I sucked in a shaky breath, trying not to move.

Another ragged grunt escaped his throat. His eyes burned, watching the way I gasped and shook. "Take me in, baby."

Spasms shook my body, inevitably nudging him deeper. Which sent another devastating ripple of sensation through me. I wanted him seated deep and hard inside me, but trepidation made me quake again. Which only allowed him to glide deeper. A vicious, shattering circle.

I fisted my hands in the bedding, trying to control myself. Even though part of me wanted to shove my hips up hard and fast. Insanity. I couldn't. Take him. Too much. I couldn't. Breathe. He took up all the space in my body, as if his dick rearranged my organs to make room. Not even a molecule of air could fit in my lungs.

Panic washed over me. Blackness filled my vision. Maybe I was going to pass out. My heart thudded. My ears roared with the sound of blood rushing through my veins.

"Breathe." He growled against my ear, a deep, vicious rumble that still somehow managed to be tender and soft. "That's it. Take me to the hilt. Such a good little human. So good. So tasty. Makes me want to take a nice, juicy bite."

A sound escaped my lips. Part gasp. A bleat of fear. A moan. Because it was so good. He covered me, his skin blazing hot against me. Massive rock and muscle, so heavy and terrifyingly large. Yet he didn't hurt me.

Even his threat to bite me only made me moan, automatically turning my head to give him my neck. Some instinctual mating ritual long dead for humans—but some remnant remained, brought back to life by him.

"Let me see your eyes."

Turning my head back, I blinked, trying to do as he asked. I stared up into inhuman red eyes. Shaking from head to foot, but also comforted. His eyes were strange, yes, but otherwise, he looked the same. He hadn't changed into the lizard thing or sprouted scales or a tail. At least not that I could see. He wasn't mindlessly ravaging me like a beast.

Though truth be told…

I'd like that. Someday. Maybe not this first time though. Not when I swore that I could feel his pulse in my abdomen.

"How does that feel?"

My brain didn't seem to be connected to my mouth. All I could manage to say was, "Ng."

One corner of his lips quirked up briefly but his jaw remained tight. Sweat dripped down his face and neck, his shoulders corded with strain. "That was the easy part."

Oh shit. Gulp.

"You trust me?"

Duh. I rolled my eyes and managed to get my mouth to work. "You have to ask that now?"

"I'll do my best to stay in control but heat rides me hard. I don't think I'll shift. But if I do, don't run. Whatever you do. Please. Don't run. I won't hurt you, but a dynos loves a good chase. I don't want to traumatize my pretty little human mate."

I rolled my eyes again though his words made heat flush my cheeks. I'd never called myself pretty. I was smart, professional, and sometimes, I could convince myself that I was cute. But pretty? Never. That was too close to beautiful, which had never, ever been an adjective used to describe me.

He leaned down, his eyes slitted. "Whatever you're thinking, I don't like it. Not one bit."

Turning his head slightly, he rubbed his forehead and temple against my cheek. Down into my throat. Up beneath my chin. As if he was rubbing his scent into my skin. Marking me like a cat.

His musky scent wasn't so strange now. I caught myself rubbing my cheek and mouth back against him, not minding the liquid on his skin. My lips tingled. It wasn't sweat, but I wasn't sure what it was. It didn't taste bad at all. A spicy aftertaste lingered on my tongue, spreading down my throat. I wasn't even aware that I'd swallowed whatever it was. That my mouth was open on his cheek, my tongue swirling over his skin the same way he'd feasted on me earlier.

He rose on his elbows. His chest heaved as he slowly hauled himself out of me. An endless, torturous pull and glide that made me writhe and gasp and claw at his back. With a heavy grunt, he shoved back inside me. A hard, controlled stroke that drove me down into the bed, crushing me beneath his weight. That massive dick cut through my body like a hot knife through butter, pushing impossibly deep. Thudding up inside me hard enough that my breath exploded out in a strangled cry.

His jaw tightened, his forehead dropping down against mine. "Recalculating."

I had no idea what that meant. He pulled back again for another thrust. I braced, my heart thudding heavily, but he didn't slam against my cervix this time.

"Better?"

The word didn't even make sense. I'd already come so hard and long that none of my other sexual encounters even measured up. Another heavy thrust wiped away every man that I'd ever known. Obliterated them into dust. His scent in my head. His body straining against me. Filling me up, impossibly wide and thick and long. I lost the ability to breathe again. To think.

He made a deep, feral growl every time he thrust that kept my instincts ping-ponging between flight or fight. Run. Struggle. Scream. I wasn't scared. Just overwhelmed with sensation. My throat hurt but I couldn't stop crying out. I flailed at his chest and shoulders, not even sure why. I didn't want him to stop. It was just too much.

Can't. Take it. Much longer.

Something cut through the haze, bringing me back with a jolt. Teeth. On my throat. He gripped me in his mouth, pressing down hard enough to make my heart thunder even faster. I froze, my mind hopping around frantically. Rip out my throat. Shred my skin. Too sharp. Those teeth didn't feel the same as when I'd kissed him. Not that I'd been running my tongue around to measure his incisors.

A rattling, snarling sound vibrated against my neck. Low.

Vicious. The sound a lion might make, guarding its kill. Right before it ripped off the choicest bits for itself.

Warmth flooded me. For a moment, I could only think that I was bleeding. That he'd torn my carotid open. But the warmth was *inside*, not on my skin. He shook against me, still making that feral sound that raised the hairs up and down my arms. And it dawned on me. Finally.

That flood was cum. So hot, in such a large quantity, that I could actually feel it dripping from my vagina down my ass crack.

Holy shit. Maybe he was right. Maybe my birth control shot didn't have a chance in hell against that much semen.

How did I feel about that?

Shellshocked to say the least. But right now, basking in the bliss of climaxing so hard and long, I couldn't bring myself to worry.

I'd dreamed of having hot, wild sex with a stranger. Of having a gorgeous man pick me up and toss me down on his bed. Things like that didn't happen to me.

Until now.

The grip of his jaws loosened on my throat. I could feel the sting where his teeth had pricked my skin, though the small pain eased as he licked and kissed the marks he'd left.

Still panting, he asked, "You okay?"

Shyness cringed through me, making it hard to meet his eyes. At least they weren't glowing like red lamps. Maybe it'd been my imagination? "Yeah."

I waited for him to get up. Roll over. Maybe be a gentleman and hand me a tissue. Actually, as messy as I felt right now, I'd need the whole box. Better yet, the shower. But he stayed on top of me, his beefy forearms bracketed on either side of my head. His mouth close enough I could feel the hot pant of his breath.

The intense scrutiny of his eyes from inches away made my cheeks burn. "I swear your eyes were red earlier."

His chest rumbled against me. "Yeah. I warned you I might shift. I'm glad I didn't."

"Shift?" My voice broke and slipped up an octave. "Into the… lizard-thing. Right? How is that possible?"

"Not human, remember?" He brushed his mouth over mine lazily, his fingers tangling in my hair. "Ask me anything."

"Um, I don't know where to start." I laughed a little, giving him a push in the chest. "Let me go clean up and I'll come up with a list."

He didn't budge. Still draped over me, he kissed my eyelid and then my temple. "I can't move yet. We're locked together."

My brain short circuited all over again. "Like… stuck? You're *stuck* inside me?"

8

NATALIE

I squirmed, trying to wriggle out from beneath his crushing weight. Holy fuck. My lungs seized and I froze. He was still inside me. As hard and big as ever. Tremors cascaded through me.

How? He'd come twice in less than an hour. He couldn't still have an erection. Could he?

A fresh shock of adrenaline-laced pleasure richoted through my body.

"Be still." He hissed against my ear. "Or I'll go for round two before you've had a chance to adjust to me."

Trembling, I balled my hands up into fists against his chest, still pushing at him. Irrational, I knew. I had no hope of budging him. He was too big. Too strong. But panic pulsed through me.

Stuck. We're stuck together. What if his dick is permanently welded inside me?

He gathered me up against him, one hand pressing my face against his chest, the other holding my shoulders as he rolled over onto his back. His chest heaved beneath me, catching on another groan. But at least I could move and breathe without giant muscles suffocating me.

I shifted, trying to get my knees under me so I could heave myself up, but pressure strained inside me. It felt like his dick had swelled up even bigger, tugging uncomfortably. Like if I moved too quickly... all my organs would be dragged out along with his dick.

His hands clamped down hard on my thighs, trying to hold me still. But more concerning—his eyes flared red again. "Fuck. Are you trying to kill me? Talk to me, baby. Distract me with your questions."

My heartbeat skipped and jumped, a frantic, uneven rhythm of sheer panic. I didn't want him to shift into the Godzilla thing. Especially now. Just the thought of feeling scales against me rather than his rock-hard body made my blood pressure rachet even higher. "How long will you be stuck?"

"It varies." His breathing was still ragged. "First time, could be quite a while."

"Why? Why is this happening?"

He ground his jaws together, muscles flinching across his cheeks. "I told you I was in heat. The knot ensures more of my semen stays inside you, increasing the chance of conception. Don't you have animals that knot here on Earth?"

"Wolves," I said faintly. "Dogs. I'm not sure about any others. You're *knotted*? Inside me?"

Now that I wasn't trying to pull away, his fierce grip gentled. He stroked his hands up and down my thighs. Up over my flanks. My back. The slow, steady strokes soothed some of the tension straining in me. I tried to relax against his chest, but he was so hard and big that it was like trying to get comfy on a concrete floor.

"It's science. Biology. The better you feel, the more you'll want to fuck me, yeah? So my pheromones are meant to attract your interest. The temporin leaking from my temples is a chemical aphrodisiac meant to stimulate the female's reproductive hormones. My tongue and cock adjust to your anatomy to make the joining as pleasurable as possible for you. Again, if you're having a good time, you'll want me again, ensuring a successful breeding."

My mind whirled and buzzed with questions. I propped my elbow on his chest, bracing my chin on my hand so I could see his face. "What are you? Exactly?"

"I'm a soldier, engineered to be nearly indestructible with a mix of Sirian and Draconian DNA."

"Draconian—like a dragon? Is that why the creature looked like a giant lizard?"

He huffed out a laugh. "I suppose so, though I'm not a dragon, at least not a dragon that you would recognize. Sirius and Draco are star systems. A group of scientists gathered DNA from some of the most lethal beings known in the universe to create Dynosauros, an elite squadron of soldiers with multiple physical forms."

"D…dino…" My brain stuttered a moment. "Dinosauros. Of course! That makes sense. The creature does look like a cross between a T-Rex and a raptor."

"The creature is me," he drawled out in a low, husky voice. "I'm the creature. Dynos. When I shift, I'm still me. I'm in full control of my intellect. Well, mostly. The predator can still be triggered by a chase, but I'm able to reason and think. I understand speech, but I'm also able to read subtle indicators that you're not even aware of. Heart rate, for example. Body temperature. Plus all my natural senses are increased with cybernetic enhancements."

"I thought I saw patterns flashing in your eyes before."

He nodded. "I carry all kinds of implants, including some in my eyes." He blinked and red circles flashed across his pupils briefly. "I can see through most carbon-based materials and detect heat signatures."

This was getting weirder by the minute, but the more he told me, the more intrigued I became. There was a reason that I'd loved shows like *Terminator* and *Battlestar Galactica*. "But how did our dinosaurs get pulled into some galactic laboratory?"

"Where do you think your dinosaurs came from in the first place?"

"But... They all died out. They're extinct. Did they do some kind of *Jurassic Park* extraction?"

His mouth quirked. "Did they die? Or did they merely go home?"

My mouth hung open a moment before I could get my brain to work again. "But... But that was like sixty-five *million* years ago."

He shrugged. "Time is meaningless once you master interstellar travel. Moving through time is the same as moving across galaxies. It's just a different kind of jump."

I couldn't help but huff out a half-strangled laugh. "So you're a time-traveling alien super-soldier who can shift into a dinosaur."

"Pretty much."

More questions popped into my head quicker than I could even formulate them into words. My brain felt like it was on fire. I'd fallen through a rabbit hole—into a science-fiction comic book where everything was possible. Even huge dino-monsters who turned into muscled, gentle giants with the stamina of a robot. "Are you a cyborg?"

He rocked his hips up beneath me, making my eyes roll back into my head. My head fell back, and I shuddered as all my nerve endings screamed with sensation. "Does that feel like a machine to you?"

KROKTL

I never imagined that I'd be sharing top-secret details of my squad's existence while my dick was locked inside the tightest, sweetest pussy in the universe. She made a soft, fragile sound that made me want to roll her beneath me and see how much deeper I could get. If we could stay locked together for hours. Days. Forever. That'd be fine by me.

"Impossible," she whispered.

I wondered for a moment if I'd spoken my thoughts out loud. "What?"

She made another low, sweet sound, her muscles clenching around my intrusion. "How can I want to start all over again?"

Mesmerized, I watched the way she quivered, restlessly shifting in a futile effort to ease the fullness she must feel. Her soft, full breasts swayed, begging for my touch. Her skin incredibly fragile, soft as down. She dug her nails into my stomach, her pussy clenching and grinding on my dick while she made those fucking hot whimpers.

I'll kill anyone and anything that threatens to take her away from me.

Her hips shimmied and squirmed, making me clench my hands on her thighs. I fought the urge to tumble her beneath me. To fuck her long and hard until she passed out senseless with pleasure, filled to the brim with cum. Vicious instinct roared inside me. *Ensure she carries my offspring. Keep her filled. Make her mine, mine, mine. Over and over and over.*

But she was human. She'd already been through a scare in the jungle, and though her natural curiosity and bright mind led her to ask a dozen questions, I didn't want to give her a reason to flee. I especially didn't want her to fear the reality of what I am. Sweat and temporin burned in my eyes, but I forced myself to lie there and take whatever she chose to give me.

No matter how much I wanted to roar and snarl and mark her delectable throat with my teeth again.

The swollen knot kept her from moving too much, acting as a plug inside her. There wasn't any thrusting or friction involved. Just agonizing squirms. The fierce grip of her pussy, muscles squeezing and quivering around me. Every inch of my dick throbbed with the need to get deeper. Claim every inch of her. I could see and feel the intricate, delicate flow of her anatomy. The barrier to her womb. The sacks where her eggs waited. I didn't sense that she was fertile this very moment, though the dynos didn't give a damn. With enough temporin and pheromones and cum spilled inside her, she'd be round with my seed soon enough.

I didn't know what such offspring would even look like— but my instincts insisted it was possible.

The bulging head of my cock throbbed, swelling up even more. I gritted my teeth, fighting to hold back another climax. Not until she'd had her pleasure. I smoothed my palms up the front of her body, testing her erogenous zones. Her breasts were tender, the tips rock hard against my palms. A ragged moan escaped her lips when I applied a little more pressure, especially on her nipples. So I leaned up and captured one in my mouth again. Gripping the soft flesh, abrading the tip with my tongue while she writhed.

Whimpered again. Panted. "Kroktl."

My name on her tongue drove me insane. I drove my hips up, lifting her off the mattress with the force of my thrust. The knot prodded at her inner barrier, and she twitched in my arms. A strangled cry escaped her throat. Her pussy locked down on me so tight that I couldn't hold back the surge of release that poured through me. Wave after wave, pumping her full, spraying her insides with semen. Only then did the swelling go down, though my cock didn't slide free yet. I wanted to stay inside her as long as possible. As long as she'd let me.

Shaking, she nestled against my chest, her head beneath my chin. Her back heaved, her muscles quivering with exertion. I could smell the dip in her blood sugar. Not urgent yet, but she would need to eat. Soon. Though I gauged the best thing for her right now would be sleep.

She groaned and tried to lift her head, though she flopped back down against me as if her bones couldn't support the weight of her head. "I need to clean up."

I rubbed my mouth on her head. "Later. Rest now."

"I'm sticky and... gross." She groaned again, though this time with bliss as I applied a bit more pressure on her muscles. Urging her to rest. "I stink of sex."

I let out a low, soothing rumble. "No, baby. You stink of me. Keep my scent and cum on you as long as possible."

"Women should pee," She mumbled. "After sex. Infection."

I huffed out a laugh. "That's one of the perks of having sex with me, then. I guarantee my sperm won't let anything else grow in you."

Except my seed.

I didn't say the last words out loud for fear it would scare her. To my knowledge, humans hadn't mated with dyni before. But after our doomed mission to Earth, it had become painfully obvious that we soldiers were on a need-to-know basis, and the higher-ups in charge obviously didn't want us to know shit.

Or we'd never have ended up stranded here.

9

KROKTL

Gazing down at my sleeping mate, I fought the urge to crawl back into bed and bury my face between her thighs again. She had to be sore, despite my adjustments to make our joining as pleasurable as possible for her. I'd filled her up tight, slamming as deeply as I could go. Then held her on top of me while she slept. The thin, old mattress was still softer than me, but I hadn't been able to let her slide down beside me.

It was a testament to her exhaustion that she slept so deeply that she hadn't woken even as I crawled out from beneath her limp body.

Which could be a massive security issue.

I needed to leave for supplies and scout the area to make sure the smugglers hadn't picked up her trail. Or the worthless humans who'd left her stranded in the first place. I could move effortlessly through the jungle as dynos, but it'd still take me at least an hour or two to secure food and make sure we were still well hidden.

Meanwhile, I'd have to leave my sleeping, vulnerable mate alone.

Even now, she could carry my offspring. I breathed deeply, mouth cracked open to take as much of her scent into my body as possible. I didn't sense fertilization but it was just a matter of time. My dynos wouldn't have been so eager to fuck her if we weren't compatible, let alone claim her as mate.

Heat still surged in my veins, but now the possessive urge to protect her also hammered at the base of my skull. There were too many threats and unknowns. I had too many enemies who'd relish hurting her to get to me. Even a member of my squad—which was the only family I'd ever known—had betrayed us.

No human could ever help me defend her as well as a Dynosauros soldier, but I might have to kill the entire squad to keep her. If they'd come into heat too—which was likely, since squad members tended to sync up their cycles—they might try to take her from me. It wasn't uncommon for an entire squad to be eliminated in a breeding frenzy if they weren't isolated.

Brutal fights to the death for the right to mate might not even leave me standing at the end. I had no doubt that I would come out on top—but I might be too damaged to care for her. Then what would happen to her?

Especially if she carried my young.

She'd need proper medical care. Not fucking human medics with their barbaric weaponry they called surgery. Snryx was the best medic in the galaxy, but could I trust him anywhere near her?

Worse, Earth had a terrible reputation for torturing and experimenting on captured extraterrestrials. I could only imagine what they'd do to her, let alone an alien embryo. If they knew humans could breed with aliens…

A silent snarl twisted my lips. I had to find a way to stay alive so I could protect her. Build her a nest somewhere safe.

Better yet, get her off planet entirely. But for that, I'd have to trust Axxol not to betray us again. Our pilot was the reason we were stranded on Earth in the first place. No fucking way could I let him anywhere near my mate.

Or I might never see her again.

Though the *best* way to protect her... would be if my entire squad was as dedicated to her as me. At least the ones I trusted. Four dyni mates, indestructible soldiers at her side. Nothing would ever harm her. As long as we didn't kill each other, Axxol didn't track us down to finish us off, and we managed to either get off planet or find a way to stay hidden on Earth indefinitely.

Would my little human mate even be willing to allow four alien monsters, as she called us, to share her?

NATALIE

Waking up alone was both a huge disappointment—and a relief. I pushed up on my elbows and glanced around the hut. Even without him, the one-room shack seemed incredibly tiny and pretty rough. The bed—barely larger than a twin— was basically a box on cement blocks with a light sheet. The mattress seemed to be made up of thin cushions for outdoor furniture. Old, tattered mosquito netting had been tacked up overhead and pushed aside like a curtain. No way would that old holey thing keep out any mosquitoes.

I could only imagine future scientists finding a fossilized mosquito in amber from our time period, wondering why it had dino-DNA. Huffing out a laugh, I gingerly sat up on the edge of the bed. I ached all over, whether from sleeping on such a thin mattress, the numerous falls I'd taken in my run through the jungle, or the extracurricular activities with Kroktl. Likely all the above.

Remembering, I rubbed my eyes, fighting down the urge to laugh hysterically and maybe cry. *What the hell are you doing, Nat?*

It wasn't like me to hook up with some random guy I'd just met. Fine. Cool. I'd been more than willing to hop into bed with him.

But he wasn't human.

He's an alien! Who shifts into an even scarier lizard-monster that chased me through the jungle!

And I still slept with him.

My hips and groin ached. Remembering his size. The way he'd stretched and filled me. The fucking knot swelled up like a basketball inside me.

Oh god.

He'd been literally stuck. IN ME. So thick and huge and long that I couldn't breathe or move without climaxing again. Just remembering...

Heat spread across my face and down my neck. Flushed, sweaty, and yeah, turned on. If he'd been here right now, I'd be climbing on for round two. Or was it three? Did the second time count because he'd still been stuck inside me?

My hand quivered as I swiped my hair out of my face. *Get a grip. Pull yourself together before he comes back.*

I pushed up to my feet, wavering as my muscles whimpered. My calves and thighs ached. My back was tight. My hips felt loose in their sockets. Fucking hell. I knew why too. Strained wide apart by his shoulders while he'd licked me...

A small grunt escaped my lips. My pussy tightened and pulsed rhythmically. My heart thudded heavily, and I bent over, bracing my hands on my knees. Waiting for it to pass.

Climax. Just thinking about him. Without a single touch.

Chills crept down my spine. Ironically, that scared me more than anything else.

I could count on one hand the number of men who'd been able to make me climax once. But for a man to give me an orgasm just thinking about him…? That was absolutely crazy.

Heat pulsed through me. My cheeks felt flushed, my eyes hot and dry. Maybe I had a fever. Wouldn't be unexpected after being in the jungle a few days, right? Though I'd gotten all my immunizations before the trip. Straightening gingerly, I concentrated on my breathing, trying to slow my heart rate down.

A lot could be going on with me right now. I might have malaria or some other insect-borne disease. I was certainly dehydrated. I hadn't eaten anything since the candy bar I'd indulged in yesterday. I'd also been through strenuous activity—not even counting wild sex with an alien lizard-man. Food, water, and a shower would fix a lot, though glancing around, I wasn't sure the latter would be possible.

There was a set of café-style swinging door opposite the main entrance. I took a peek and nearly wept with relief. A tiny, dark bathroom complete with a cramped shower. I wasn't sure about the water source, and the water wasn't hot, but washing away the grime and sweat made me feel like a new woman. The cool water soothed my heated skin. It was too gloomy in the tiny shower to tell, but I expected my legs to be covered in scratches from my panicked flight through the jungle. I sudsed my lower legs well, hoping any cuts didn't get infected, though nothing stung and I didn't feel any scabs.

I couldn't find a towel so I let myself air dry. My hair was so tangled that I was afraid I'd just have to hack it all off. I didn't want to snoop too much through his personal things to look for deodorant or a comb but I did find a stack of faded T-shirts folded on a rickety shelf by the bed. The shirt smelled a bit musty but seemed fairly clean, though it was much too small for him. Maybe it belonged to the shack's previous owner? Did an alien even wear clothes or have basic toiletries? How long had he been here?

When was he going back…?

Just the thought of him leaving made my stomach pitch and roll.

Red flag. Why would I care? I barely knew the man. We'd had great sex, sure, but I couldn't possibly be romantically attached to him already. He hadn't told me much at all about how he'd gotten to Earth, when or how he would leave, what life was like back on his planet. All I knew was that he'd been stranded here after some kind of rescue mission, though the way he'd hesitated told me that was just the tip of the iceberg.

The little kitchen consisted of a mini fridge and a hotplate on a rusted rolling cart. Fresh bananas sat on top of the hotplate. I didn't remember them being there last night, but I hadn't exactly been observant of anything but the ginormous dick swinging in front of me.

My pussy clenched again and I quickly pushed any thoughts about his physique away. I didn't need another hands-off climax, thank you very much. I was still weirded out by the other one. My mouth watered looking at the fruit, so I decided to help myself to a banana and a bottle of water from the fridge. He'd given me one last night. I didn't think he'd mind. If he did…

Then I'd know exactly what kind of asshole I was dealing

with. I'd have the excuse I needed to book it for camp as quickly as I could go.

I sat cross-legged on the bed since there weren't any chairs. My stomach quivered with ecstasy on the food and water, though unease still wriggled through my brain. It took me a minute to put my finger on the anxiety. Camp. I didn't know where it was. I had no idea where this cabin was. If he didn't want to let me leave…

Where would I go? I couldn't call for help unless he managed to find my backpack. What if he found it—and destroyed my phone? Threw it in a river or tossed it in a ravine? Even if he gave it to me, would it have a charge? Would I have enough signal to get through to Holly or Dr. Snyder? Even if I did, how would I tell them my location?

I had no clothes, map, phone, laptop, or contact with any other human… I had no idea where I was even if I managed to reach help.

I'm fucked. And not in the good way.

10

NATALIE

I didn't hear him approaching. There weren't any heavy footsteps to alert me. The door opened and there he was, suddenly filling up the tiny shack. Wide eyed, I stared at him like a deer frozen in approaching headlights. He seemed so much bigger in broad daylight. His head nearly touched the ceiling. Everything bulged. Massive arms. Beefy chest and shoulders.

I'm not looking further south...

I didn't even have the chance to peek at his dick again because he advanced too quickly. One moment he was by the door. The next he loomed over me, hands planted on either side of me, red eyes glittering like faceted rubies. Oh shit. Did that mean his creature was close?

He breathed deeply and his lips curled back in distaste. A deep, vicious rumble rolled from his chest, sending icy shards down my spine. "What the fuck is this?"

Bewildered, I glanced down my front. "A... sh... shirt. I found it." I jerked my head toward the little stand. "Over there."

He let out another growling hiss that made my heart

shudder and skip a beat before pounding into the full-blown gallop of a panic attack. "It smells like him."

"Him? Who?"

"*Him.*" He seized the front of the T-shirt in both hands and tore the cotton like it was tissue paper. "The male who lived here before. I don't like his scent on my mate."

My mind jittered frantically. "M… m… mate? Who lived here before?"

Lowering his head, he sniffed at my chest, bumping me insistently with his head until I fell back on my elbows. He rubbed his face over my breasts. My stomach. Back and forth, both sides of his head. It was odd but not overtly sexual. Sort of like a cat rubbing itself on your leg.

Of course. He was rubbing his scent onto my skin.

Up over my throat and back down the front of my body, leaving behind a glistening oil. His scent filled my nose. The strange, vaguely reptilian scent of the lizard-monster. The thing that had chased me and tossed me down in a hole. I vaguely remembered licking that weird oil off his face last night.

Heat scorched my cheeks, partly mortification that I'd been so turned on that I'd be willing to lick some weird sweat-oil sheen off a stranger's face, but also desire—to do it again. My skin warmed everywhere he rubbed, as if the oil had some kind of magical heating property. The gentle abrasion of his face against my breasts made my nipples ache for his touch. His mouth. That wicked tongue.

"Not good enough." Lifting his head, he flattened a platter-sized palm over my chest and pushed me down flat on my back. Straddling my legs, he leaned down over me, pumping his dick.

My eyes widened. I had a second to wonder how he was going to get inside me with my legs pressed together beneath him. But then the first drops of cum splashed on my stomach. My chest. Still rumbling that low, dangerous sound, he stroked his other palm over me, rubbing the semen in like it was lotion.

His scent filled me, a harsh, dangerous predator odor that was also arousing. I shivered with terror, filled with the urge to run. Curl up into a ball. Throw my hands over my head. But I ached at the same time. I'd come so easily before just thinking about him. Now I wanted to come, needed to come, but I couldn't. My pussy throbbed, tight and hot and so damned empty.

"I'd roll you over and cover your back in scent too, but I guarantee if I see that sweet ass I'll be inside you."

A sound escaped my lips. A squeaky, hiccupy moan. All too easily, I could picture him taking me doggy style. Shoving my head down into the bed. Pulling my hair. I bit my lip to keep from moaning again. When he backed off the bed and hauled me back upright, I wanted to sob with longing.

Which scared the shit of out me. How could I want him so badly, this stranger, this alien, that I knew nothing about? It wasn't reasonable and sure as fuck wasn't normal. It wasn't like me to ogle a man so openly. To let a man come on me and rub his semen into my skin like a moisturizer. And then quake with the force of my lust.

I had to be sick. Some kind of jungle fever. Stockholm's Syndrome, maybe? But he hadn't kidnapped me. Yet. Not that I knew of. He'd rescued me. From the creature. Himself.

Riiiight.

He sat on the floor beside the bed, but he still loomed over me. "You need to eat first. Your blood sugar's dangerously low. Didn't you eat some of the fruit I brought you?"

I gave myself a mental shake. I was staring at his dick again. Still hard despite the semen he'd rubbed into me. As large and thick and hard as I remembered. My pussy clenched so hard a soft grunt escaped my lips.

"Natalie?"

I focused on his eyes, narrowed with concern. "I got one of the bananas but I don't remember eating it."

He picked up the discarded banana beside me on the bed and pushed it into my hand. "Eat this first. Get some natural sugar into your body while I bring in the rest."

I stared at the fruit in my hand a moment. Trying to think. Move. I blinked back tears. "What's wrong with me?"

He peeled the banana for me and gently lifted my hand to my mouth, encouraging me to take a bite. "Nothing's wrong. You've been through a lot, and I haven't cared for you properly. That's my mistake, not yours. I'll do a better job of making sure I have appropriate food and water for you."

The sweet banana tasted so good that I couldn't hold back a moan of bliss. I couldn't remember a simple banana ever tasting so good before. Granted, by the time I bought a bunch of bananas from the grocery store, they were days if not weeks old, but I couldn't remember anything tasting so good before.

He stepped outside a moment and came back into the shack with several bags that he lay on the floor. Kneeling in front of me, he lifted my hand up to my mouth again. Silently reminding me to eat.

Tears dripped down my cheeks. If the banana was so good, and I was so hungry, why couldn't I eat it without him prompting me?

The low rumble rolled from his chest again, soothing this time instead of scary. Almost like a reptilian purr. Did lizards purr? "Eat, baby. You're safe. Nothing's going to hurt you now or ever again. Would you like to see what else I brought you?"

Swallowing another bite, I nodded. He opened a burlap

bag and rummaged around inside it. Something made my nose twitch. Spicy, warm goodness. I wasn't sure what it was, but it smelled incredible.

He pulled out a small crock and set it onto my lap. Heat radiated from it and the smells made my mouth water as he took the lid off. It looked like some kind of bean stew with chunks of vegetables and meat. I shoved the remaining banana in my mouth and picked up the crock, my hands trembling with anticipation. "What is it? Where'd you get it?"

"There's a small village a few minutes away. I don't know the name of the dish, but other humans were eating it, so it should be safe for you."

He'd even grabbed a wooden spoon, though it was a bit too large for my mouth. This time, I had no problem feeding myself without his prompting. I groaned with bliss at the first savory bite, enjoying the heat from chiles and the sweet corn and carrots. Maybe a hint of chocolate? A mole sauce. "I'm no connoisseur by any means but I've never tasted anything better in my life."

"We'll see about that, baby." He made another low, rattling sound that curled my toes. "I found your bag."

Blushing at the innuendo, it took a moment for his words to penetrate. "Oh! You did? Where was it?"

"Near the trail where you first saw me." He lifted another sack up onto the mattress beside me and dumped out my field pack. Along with my laptop and clothes—that I had left back at the base camp. "I followed your trail back to where you were staying and retrieved everything that smelled like you."

He'd even taken the coffee cup that I'd been using—even though it belonged to the cook. "Your nose is that good? I'm sure that cup has been washed several times."

"Like I said last night, now that I've had a taste of you, I'll be able to track you anywhere."

I supposed that explained his adverse reaction to the old shirt I'd borrowed from the previous owner. "How many people were in camp? Did anyone see you, or ask about me?"

Sitting on the floor, he leaned against the bed, bracing his elbow on the mattress beside me. With dark ruby eyes, he watched me eat. "Nobody sees me unless I *want* to be seen. I roared a few times and the village cleared out enough for me to grab some supplies for you. The camp was nearly empty. Just a couple of locals."

"Probably the guards. One of them was having a baby. That's why they left me at the ruin in the first place. You didn't see a stuffy prick walking around camp wringing his hands, wondering where I'd gone off to?"

"No one seemed concerned or alarmed."

My phone was in the outside pocket of the backpack. So close but so far away. I peeked at him through my lashes, trying to decide if I should risk picking it up to see if I had any calls or texts. If he would care at all. Maybe he didn't even know what it was.

Setting the crock down on the bed, I reached for the backpack as nonchalantly as possible. I unzipped the middle section first, checking to make sure my camera and map were still there. Then I pulled the phone out. I still had a little sliver of battery. No signal, though I'd received a couple of texts.

I cast another quick glance up at him, trying to gauge his reaction. And almost dropped the phone when I realized he offered the end of a charger. "You… you know what it is? And you don't mind?"

His upper lip pulled back, baring his teeth a moment. "I'm an engineered soldier enhanced with cybernetic capabilities so advanced that you wouldn't believe me if I told you all the things I can do. I've been sent on countless missions through numerous star systems with technology so advanced you'd think it's magic and wizardry. Do you really think I don't recognize a communication device? Why would I mind that you have your device in your possession?" His eyes narrowed, his voice dropping to an ominous slither. "Unless you think I'm holding you against your will, or that you're in danger with me."

I forced out a laugh and plugged the charger into my phone. "I didn't know for sure. You're… a lot. Different. You said m…mate earlier. That doesn't imply that you'd let me leave if I wanted to."

"You're free to go anywhere you'd like. Just know that I'll be right behind you."

He plugged the other end of the charger into a small black power bank, and my phone gave the charging ding. I tried to imagine him getting on an airplane with me to go back to the States. Walking across campus. Going shopping with me. This giant, naked alien soldier. Even if he didn't shift to the lizard-thing, he'd stand out like a sore thumb anywhere he went. Even with normal clothes, he would just be too big. Too… mean looking.

I cocked my head, studying him more openly with the sunshine coming through the shack's only window. At first glance, he appeared human, though abnormally large. Sort of like Dwayne Johnson, only taller and wider. The same bald head, massive, bulging shoulders and arms. Platter-sized hands that could palm my head like a basketball.

Even sitting on the floor didn't disguise his massive size. The proportions of his body were off. His arms were too long, his chest thick and barreled. One thigh was the size of an entire person. I had no idea if I could even find clothes to fit him. No hair, anywhere on his body, not even his groin or legs. The texture of his skin seemed off, somehow thicker yet shiny. In the sunlight, his coloring was a mottled grayish beige.

I looked back into his eyes, darker brown than red now. I tried picturing him sitting across from me at a restaurant, walking down the sidewalk with me to window shop, driving a car, getting a job, buying a house in suburbia somewhere. Normal things married adults did together. All the things I'd planned to do after I got my PhD and accepted a research position, hopefully somewhere in Central America.

I'd worked so hard for that future. Even dealing with Dr. Snyder's misogyny so I could get here, my first real dig that could lead to publication. Countless hours in the library. All the hours I'd worked since I could drive, saving every penny to cover the tuition and expenses that my scholarships and student loans didn't cover.

I owed a fortune. I needed a really good job.

I couldn't see that future anymore.

And it scared the shit out of me.

11

KROKTL

While I loved her eyes on me, drinking in my form, I didn't like the hesitation in her eyes, mixed with doubt and fear and uncertainty. Not one bit. My instincts roared to life, insisting I should stake my claim on her body again. Remind her thoroughly, exhaustively what I offered her. Keep her climaxing, or exhausted from climaxing, and she wouldn't doubt that I was the best possible mate for her.

But it was *mate* that seemed to alarm her the most. So a vigorous fucking probably wouldn't ease her doubts. No matter how much my beast burned with fury at the thought that she wasn't sure of me at all.

I got it. She had no idea what she was dealing with. I wasn't hiding anything from her—but I also hadn't had the opportunity to share much with her yet. An hour or two at most before she'd collapsed into post-coital exhaustion. She'd slept the hours I was away gathering supplies, though I checked on her several times in between trips.

I needed more time to prove that I could protect her. Provide for her. Give her anything in the universe that she desired. Getting hissy and aggressive with my little human wouldn't help her very justified fears. Lightly, I nudged her knee and gave a pointed look at the food she'd forgotten about. "Don't forget to eat while you check your messages."

She pulled her gaze away from me and took another bite. "Aren't you going to eat?"

"I already did."

She glanced back up at me, her brow furrowed. "Does human food not agree with you?"

Questions about my eating habits weren't going to put her fears to rest, but I refused to lie to her. "Humans, yes. Human food, no."

Her head jerked back up, blood draining from her face. "You... you do eat people. Why didn't you eat me last night when you first found me?"

She seemed to enjoy my mating sounds as long as I kept them soft and non-aggressive. "You know why, baby. As soon as I caught the first whiff of you, I had a whole different kind of eating in mind. I don't hunt humans exclusively, but when they're especially stupid and obvious prey, I take advantage of the easy kill."

Some of the blood rushed back to pinken her cheeks but her hand trembled as she lifted the spoon to her mouth. "I guess I did look a lot like a prey animal. Lost, defenseless, no weapons or anything to fight with. It was pretty stupid of me to try and walk right past you."

Another low rumble rattled up out of my throat before I could tame it. "Not stupid at all. Predators respect confidence and brains. You didn't run. You made yourself as big as possible. If you'd kept on walking, I would have let you pass me unharmed, even if you weren't my mate."

Her delicate jaw clenched a moment, and she swallowed the mouthful of food. "Explain what you mean by mate, please."

"I'm in heat, primed to breed with any compatible

females. Dyni are vicious predators, and a breeding frenzy is dangerous, especially on a mission. So we're usually given supplements to regulate our cycles until we're in a safe, controlled environment with ready breeding stock."

She grimaced. "We do stuff like that with horses and other animals. People control the breeding lines of animals, not each other."

I cocked my head. "I bet it happens with humans more than you think. It's instinctual to pick a good, compatible partner who'll make the best children. It's nature's way of continuing our species and making us better. Dyni are engineered to be the best. Each of us has a specific purpose on our squad, and we grow and develop together. I have skills that none of the other males in my squad have, and it's important that I pass those skills on to my offspring."

"How often do you come into heat? Do you already have offspring, er, children?"

"I've only come into heat three times since I first became an adult. It's necessary for males to have at least one heat cycle to fully develop our size and capacity. The breeding wasn't successful, likely by design."

Her brow furrowed. "I have so many questions. I'm afraid I'm going to forget to ask them all."

I bared my teeth in a controlled grin that she hopefully would read as pride in her intelligence and not a threat. "Ask your questions. I won't forget them and promise to answer everything with as much detail as I can provide."

"Your *size* changed after the first heat cycle? By design—like you think they controlled which woman, er, female, you were given so she wouldn't get pregnant? Who controls all this? Is dyni the lizard thing? Are females soldiers too or just males? You said a rescue mission before. How were you stranded? How many were in your squad?" She paused, her chest heaving on a gulp as she caught up on her breathing. "When will you leave?"

NATALIE

My brain buzzed with so many ideas, hopping from question to question quicker than I could even voice them. The more he told me, the more questions I had.

"My size doubled after I came into heat the first time, though the gains later weren't as significant. It'll be interesting to see how much, if any, I grow this time."

My eyes flared, my mouth sagging open at the thought. I tried to imagine the Godzilla-thing in the jungle getting even bigger and almost peed myself. "You'll grow every single time we… uh…"

He made that low rattling sound again that I was starting to recognize as amusement. "Not each time, thankfully, or I'd outgrow this planet in a hurry, though the hormones continue to change my physique. Heat usually only lasts a few hours once a compatible female is willing to breed. Though this first time, it might take the beast longer to settle down. I've been burning with need for weeks."

"But your heat cycles are usually controlled?"

"I've served thirty-three rotations without coming into heat. It's definitely an anomaly to have it happen now, especially with a species not previously known to be compatible with dyni. It's even rarer for dyni to mate, so the chances that I would find you were one in a trillion."

I took another bite of the delicious stew, making myself chew slowly while I thought. He seemed so earnest. So convinced that I was special. And yeah, that was a terrific feeling. He wanted me. I'd never been the girl the hot guy wanted, let alone with such single-minded intensity.

But *mate*…?

I wasn't ready for a husband in any way, shape, or form. That had never been part of my life plan.

I flicked my gaze up to his face, not surprised to see him watching me eat, as if it was as entertaining as a new club on the Vegas Strip.

"You're so special and rare, baby," he murmured with the low, rattling purr. "You have no idea, do you? These fucking human males are absolutely useless. Dyni rarely come into heat, but it's even rarer for us to mate. I don't think a dyni has mated for generations. I knew you were mine as soon as I smelled you. Seeing you only made me want you more."

My cheeks heated. His words made me want to squirm like a cute, wriggly puppy. I didn't think I had a praise kink but if he told me I was his good girl I'd probably die on the spot. Hot, pulsing tingles tightened my pussy. If I wasn't careful, I'd come again just sitting here, like I had earlier today.

Naked. On the bed. My legs crossed, which exposed me to his gaze. It'd be so easy to just lie back and open my thighs. Invite him to dive in again. His tongue stroking me. Curling inside me. Impossibly long—

Tremors rippled through me. My breath caught, holding back a soft gasp. Fucking hell. I'd done it again. I'd actually managed to make myself climax just thinking about him.

Mortified, I tried to cover up my reaction by lifting a shaking hand to my mouth with another bite. "Mate," I rasped out, trying to make my tongue connect to my brain. "Heat. Isn't that the same thing?"

A wave of his musky scent swept over me so strongly that I could taste him on my tongue despite the chili heat in the stew.

"Heat and mate are two entirely different things."

His voice rumbled so deep and rough that I risked another quick look at his face. His nostrils flared, his eyes glowing red like hellfire forges. He'd told me before that he could sense body temperature changes and even heart rate. Of course he knew that I'd just climaxed a foot away without him even lifting a finger. To his credit, he didn't touch me or even inch closer, though his shoulders rippled with corded tendons. As if he was braced to pounce.

"Heat means I want to fuck you. Fill you up with my cum. Over and over until you're carrying my offspring."

Gulp. I swallowed hard and almost choked on the stew. I could only stare at him, trembling beneath the onslaught of heat and need pulsing through my body. My pussy ached, empty and wet and ready to feel that merciless stretch as he filled me.

He paused, drawing in a deep, rattling breath. Lips parted, his tongue stroking over his lips as if he could taste me on the air. "Mate is all of that and more. Mate means I'll never come in heat for another female. Ever. Mate means you're my only priority. Fuck the mission. Fuck the squad. Fuck Dynosauros. Fuck Earth. Fuck it all. You come first."

With a surge so fast he seemed to blur, he leaned into my

space. His massive hand cupped the back of my head, fingers tangled in my hair. Hot breath wafted over my face, his lips hovering over mine. "Most importantly, you're fucking *mine*."

12

KROKTL

She had no fucking idea what she did to me. What I wanted to do to her.

Sitting there. Watching her come. Smelling her rising heat. Tasting her cream on the air. She hungered for me. Needed me. It was pure agony to sit here and deny her, though I must worry about her health as well as her desire. But now that I was touching her, I couldn't focus on anything but her delectable scent.

"You should eat more," I growled out, fighting the urge to throw the crock of human food aside and bury my face in the honeyed heat of her body.

She made a pained sound that cut through some of the haze clouding my brain. "I couldn't eat another bite."

I did a quick scan, evaluating my grip on her head. Not too tight. I didn't press her beneath me, crushing an organ or impeding her breathing. I hadn't even thought about penetrating her yet. But she did feel pain. I shifted around so I could sit on the mattress and pull her into my lap. I cupped her face in my palms and blinked, shifting my eyes to infrared. Her temperature was slightly elevated, but that could be the environment. Or the fact that she'd just climaxed.

I blinked again, shifting my vision to look deeper into her tissues.

"Your eyes," she breathed out. "What are you doing?"

"You hurt. I'm scanning your body to determine the cause." I lifted her up higher, letting her dangle in my grip so I could scan her chest cavity. "Are you ill? Did the food not agree with you?"

She squirmed in my grip. "Put me down. I'm fine."

Ignoring her protests, I gave her a toss and caught her ass in my other hand, shifting her to lie horizontally in front of me so I could slowly roll her over for a deeper scan of her organs.

"Kroktl!" She jerked in my grip, her cheeks red. "Please."

Immediately, I ceased the examination, though concern still niggled through me. "Are you sure? It's a risk but I can contact Snryx if you need medical aid."

"I'm sure. I can tell you what it was. It's just… embarrassing. Who's Snryx?"

"He's the medic of my squad. There's no embarrassment between mates. If you have a need, I will meet it. Even if that means bringing another dynos into your vicinity."

Her eyes widened. "You mentioned your squad before, but I assumed they were dead or… gone back, I guess. They're still here? Where? How many?"

I gripped her chin and narrowed my eyes. "First, explain the pain."

"Uh, sure. It's dumb, really. Certain foods…" Her cheeks remained red but she straightened her shoulders and took on an analytical tone. "Certain foods generate harmless gas in my stomach, which can cause pain. It's not serious."

"What foods?"

"There were beans in the stew. They're very good and

healthy to eat—but they can make my stomach hurt temporarily."

I frowned. Feeding my human mate was going to be more difficult than I thought. Too bad I couldn't just kill something for her. "How can they be good and healthy to eat if they cause you pain? What else should you avoid?"

"The only thing I'm allergic to is shellfish. I should have an epi-pen in my bag."

I made a mental note, though I had no idea what shellfish were or what an epi-pen was. If I dared access Lohr on the grid, our squad biologist could help me identify her allergens with a thought. "Then you should have the bag close at all times?"

She nodded sheepishly. "Yeah, unless I lose it again. Tell me about your squad."

With my naked, luscious mate sitting in my lap, the last thing I wanted to talk about were the other males in my squad, but I'd made a promise. "There are five dyni per squad. Each soldier has a different specialty designation, enhanced by both training and breeding for centuries. In your language, I'd be called a Tri-R, valued for my speed, agility, and cunning."

"Tri-R? What does that stand for? Is it the kind of creature you are or something else?"

"Red Raptor Rex. I'm usually the point, the furthest out in the field from the rest of the squad. I'm a tracker and striker. In and out before anyone even knows I'm there."

Her eyes lit up. "Raptor! Of course. The creature did look like a cross between a T-Rex and velociraptor. And the medic? What's his designation?"

"SPR, Special Rex, though his breed is also spiny, so the SP works for that too."

"Sp...spiny? Like a... Spinosaurus?"

My head tipped slightly. "If they have a fan of spines that run down their backs, sure."

"Plus Tyrannosaurus Rex." Her eyes widened, her mouth soft and luscious. "The king of dinosaurs. Though I think we've discovered some that were bigger than that."

My jaws clenched, a muscle ticking across my cheek. "Yeah. There are."

She brushed her knuckles over my face, her brow creasing. "What's wrong?"

"Every Dynosauros squad leader is designated BGR, Blue Gig Rex, the biggest, baddest dynos ever created. But our squad leader had a few additional modifications."

"Gig… Like giganotosaurus?" Shaking her head, she laughed though I didn't sense any humor in her manner. "I can't believe I'm talking about extinct dinosaurs in present tense. I'm an archaeologist not a paleontologist, for fuck's sake. If your squad leader is bigger and badder than you, then I don't think my puny human brain could bear seeing it. Him. Whatever. I'd be scared shitless."

"Good. You should be."

Her eyes flared and she sat up a little straighter. "Why?"

"He's a fucking traitor. If you see him, we're dead."

NATALIE

I hadn't even known this man twenty-four hours yet. *Man*? Ha. He wasn't a human male at all. An alien shapeshifting soldier who ran around the jungle in a formidable monstrous form that was the stuff of nightmares. If he said we'd die if his squad leader showed up...

"What happened?" I asked, trying not to let my teeth chatter.

"We're not exactly sure," he admitted, his mouth a grim, harsh slant. "We were sent to Earth on a seemingly routine mission. Should've been a quick, easy in and out."

"You said a rescue mission before."

Some of the grimness eased from his mouth as he quirked his lips. "That was the easiest way for me to explain it without terrifying you even more. We were here to rescue Earth by killing something else. I didn't know if that would make you trust me even less or not."

"Some*thing* else?"

He nodded. "There are millions of sentient species across the multiverse. Most of them work together at least in their own galaxies or federations to protect their planets and aren't considered a danger to others. Some are more warlike than others, don't get me wrong, but they're not considered lethally dangerous. They don't wipe out entire civilizations just because they can. But there are some species for which killing is their entire existence. They literally can't breed if they're not killing, and when they find new grounds, we have to act fast."

My stomach clenched—and it had nothing to do with the beans. "These killer types were here?"

"Not confirmed. We found wreckage but no sign of spawn. We reported our findings to HQ. They ordered us to return to Nyan Station."

Softly, he smoothed his palm over my hair in gentle pets. Not to soothe me, I sensed—but to soothe himself. "Was that a bad thing?"

"Nyan Station is for decommissioning." He sighed, his eyes flickering with red flashes. "It certainly wasn't expected. Dyni squads usually operate for a hundred cycles or more before they're decommissioned. Axxol took matters into his own hands and went off grid. Without him, we can't leave the planet."

"Why would he do that? Was he under some kind of investigation?"

Kroktl blew out another sigh, this one deeper like his beast's rattling purr. "Possibly. He shut down the grid before we could question him. He almost killed Lohr when he tried to track him. We decided the best thing we could do was split up, lay low, and wait for another dyni squad to come. Though now that we've been off the grid so long, HQ probably assumes we're all working with Axxol. That we're all traitors."

I didn't like the sound of that. "If they think you're all working together… Will the other squad attack? What about when you get back to the station?"

He drew me closer. Spreading his palm wide, he ran his massive hand up and down my spine. "I've been in these jungles for months and haven't seen any sign of my own squad, let alone another. As long as I stay off grid, they won't find us easily."

So many questions whirled in my head. When I'd first woke up today, I'd imagined going back to my old life. I could say I'd been lost in the jungle for a couple of days. No big deal. Kroktl could take me to the village he'd mentioned, or a bigger town. In my head, that had still been an option.

But if bad guys were coming… Another squad of super soldier killers—like him. Or this traitor of his squad. Or even the other dangerous aliens he'd come to stop in the first place. All of those threats meant one thing.

He could die.

My stomach wrenched into a vicious knot. It wasn't my heart. I couldn't say that I loved him. I'd only just met him. I didn't believe in love at first sight anyway. Half of what he'd just told me only generated more questions and concerns. But the thought of being separated from him…

Hurt. Physically. Sweat beaded on my forehead. I breathed shallowly, trying not to panic.

"Shhh, baby," he whispered against my ear. "I won't leave you. I can't. You're my mate."

Shaking, I gripped his neck. "They might kill you."

He chuckled, a deep, toe-curling laugh that slithered through my belly and started to loosen the painful knots in a wash of heat. "They can try, but they won't succeed. Not while I have you to protect."

13

NATALIE

I felt so small in his arms. Small and safe and cherished. Me. The bigger girl who'd always been picked last for anything that didn't involve my brain. He picked me up and moved me around like I was a delicate, precious thing he'd break if he squeezed too hard.

Which honestly was probably true. His massive hands were so powerful, his shoulders impossibly wide, his biceps thick. If he flexed too hard, he could pop my head like a melon. He wouldn't have to shift to the creature to rip me limb from limb.

But he wouldn't. I didn't know much about him, not really, but I knew without a shadow of a doubt that he wouldn't ever deliberately hurt me. My brain still shivered and flinched at the thought of the monster in the jungle. But the man? Never.

And there was so much man. Bulging muscle everywhere I touched. His skin burned with heat, radiating his musky scent even more. Cradled on his lap, I was engulfed by his size and strength. I flattened my breasts against the broad expanse of his chest, soaking him in. The closer I got to him, my body touching his, the more the knots in my stomach eased.

It terrified me how much I wanted him. Needed him. Already, just one day in, I couldn't stop thinking about sex. I'd climaxed twice without him even touching me. I reeked of his cum, yet all I could think about was seeing how much more he could put in or on me.

Damn. That was fucked up. In a million years, I'd never have guessed that I'd want a man to jizz all over me and rub it into my skin. Or come inside me again and again, leaving me sticky and—

My brain wanted to say gross. But my pussy quivered on the verge of climax again.

He let out a soft grunt. "Climb on my dick before you come again, baby. Let me feel your sweet pussy squeezing me."

Gripping his shoulders, I rose on my knees, bracing myself on his massive thighs. His cock brushed against my stomach, a red-hot iron rod. So big that it still boggled my mind that he'd managed to fit inside me. I'd have to scale his body like a mountain climber to reach the tip.

His big hands slid under my thighs, lifting me up high against his chest. No fumbling or awkward squirming needed. The broad head of his dick bumped my entrance, locked and loaded. Ready for action.

He could have slammed up into me. Dropped me down onto his massive erection, letting gravity do the work. Instead, he simply held my thighs, waiting for me to take him at my own speed.

Letting my ass drop down lower, I rubbed myself against his cock. Rolling my hips, rocking against him, letting the tip slide between my lips. Deeper, the broad head pushing inside me. Hot enough I gasped. Big enough that my heart thudded heavily. Adrenaline flooded my system. I barely had an inch of him inside me and it felt like my heart was going to explode out of my ribcage.

I panted, wriggling back and forth in his grip. "Are you… bigger?"

A deep rumble rolled from his chest, vibrating through my core. "Yeah. Probably. Hormones are a bitch." He paused for a moment. His jaw flexed and worked. Sweat beaded on his upper lip. His nostrils flared. His eyes blazed red, flashing with symbols too fast for me to read or understand. "There. Try that."

I shifted ever so slightly, and his dick glided inside me. Still hot and hard but not so impossibly broad. My breath caught in my throat, my hips dipping deeper automatically. Driven by instinct. Lust. Whatever. I had to get that glorious hard dick inside me. All the way. I groaned, pushing him deeper, my hips undulating desperately. More. I twisted side to side, working his dick inside me as far as it could go. Now that he was inside me, he seemed to swell, filling up every nook and cranny. I couldn't help but think about the knot that had locked us together last night.

Another wave of heat poured through me. My eyes felt hot and fevered, my lips dry and cracked.

Stuffed to the brim, I still wanted more. More dick. More of his scent. His skin. His touch. I wanted him everywhere. I tried to push down harder to take him to the hilt, but white-hot flares shot through me, making me cry out.

His fingers dug into my thighs, lifting me up incrementally until the sensation eased. "Don't hurt yourself."

"I want more." I winced at my whiny tone but I couldn't help it. I couldn't sit still. I squirmed against him, pulling at his shoulders, his neck. I wanted—needed—*more*.

I pressed my mouth against his skin. Hot velvet. Thick muscle. My mouth watered, like I wanted to bite him. Like for real, I wanted to grab a hunk of him. The meat of his shoulder. And hold him in my mouth.

Which freaked me the fuck out. That wasn't normal. That wasn't me.

Was it?

He gathered me close, enfolding me against him. His shoulders and chest curled around me. One palm cradled the back of my head, his other braced my weight, his fingers digging into my buttock.

"Amazing," he breathed against my ear. "So fucking hot. You're feeling a mating instinct despite being human."

"I don't feel like myself." My voice broke on a deep, ragged groan. "I don't like it."

A hard click at my ear made me flinch. "I'm so sorry, Natalie. I'll make it up to you or die trying. I can't leave you unless I'm dead."

"No, that's not what I meant." I rubbed my face against him, fighting the urge to cry and wail. "I just feel so… so… inferior."

Another harsh clang at my ear made all the hairs stand up on my arms. He gripped my chin and jerked my face up, his eyes glittering like red rubies. "What the fuck? How could you possibly think that you're fucking inferior? I already told you how rare it is for us to mate. Don't you understand? They don't fucking *want* us to mate. They don't want us to breed on our own outside in the wild. Everything is controlled down to when we even come into heat. They never would have sent a squad to Earth if they'd known even the slightest probabilities that you existed. *You*, Natalie. You are a priceless, indescribably rare and precious thing that I'll exterminate this entire planet to keep."

"But I can't even take you all the way inside," I whispered, my voice quivering. I wanted to curl into a tiny ball of shame and disappear. First I had gas pains, then I kept coming at the drop of a hat, which was definitely embarrassing. Now I realized that he couldn't even get inside me all the way. So fucking humiliating.

Was there literally something wrong with me? Maybe that was why I'd never had a long-term partner before. I couldn't hold men's interest for long.

That sharp clanging sound jerked my attention up to his face. Lips peeled back, he bared his teeth. Long, sharp, shiny, vicious teeth. "Do you honestly think your worth is tied to the depth of your cunt? I want you even if you don't have a hole for me to use. As long as you're feeling pleasure, I don't care what the fuck we do. I'll lay on my back and let the cum spray out of my body so you can wallow on me however you wish. I want *you*. Your scent. Your touch. Every cell in my body is tuned to you now. I resonate when you're near, and the closer I am to you, the better I feel. I need *you*. Physically near, touching me, your scent in my nostrils. Without you, I'm dead. Literally. I'm mated to you, now. If I lose you, I'll die. If you die, so will I. I can't live without you."

Tears burned my eyes, my throat tight. He wasn't making a declaration of love—only biology. But I'd never heard such vehemence and reverence ringing in a man's voice before. "You don't mind that I'm human?"

He pressed his face to mine, nose to nose, forehead to forehead. "You don't mind that I'm a big lizard-thing with ginormous claws and red eyes?"

I couldn't help but laugh, though tears leaked from my eyes too. "I did call you a lizard."

"Yet here I am, buried in the snuggest pussy in the universe, and you're mine, every delightful inch of you."

I still had a niggling regret that I couldn't take him balls deep, but he did have a point about me being snug. Watching his face, I deliberately squeezed my vagina around that glorious dick.

His jaws worked back and forth, and a fresh line of sweat trickled down his forehead. "Are you trying to kill me, little human?"

"Maybe," I said, feeling a little more confident. "Have you ever heard of Kegels?"

His eyes narrowed to slits. "Is this something else you're allergic to or that may cause you to feel pain?"

Tension eased from my body, and I relaxed against his chest. Nuzzling my face up against his neck, I breathed in his scent. All predator, a deadly creature who could kill me with one flick of his giant claw. Yet all he cared about was whether I was hurting or safe. "Not at all. Can I try something?"

"My body is yours to command."

A thrill shot through me. I wrapped my arms around him. My thighs. Tightening my entire body around his. My palms flat on his back, my face on his throat. Eyes closed, I breathed him in and listened to the steady thunder of his pulse. Faster than mine, a deep, hard steady tempo. It made me think of a thoroughbred horse, how hard its heart must beat during a race.

I squeezed my inner muscles again, and his pulse leaped. His chest expanded beneath me in a deep breath, but he didn't otherwise move. Again. I concentrated on a rolling clench, trying to squeeze the full length inside me. Harder each time, even though it made me sweat, too. Tremors rocked through us both. Nerve endings screamed with sensation. A deep, heavy ache spread through my pussy, intensifying with each deliberate squeeze.

My breathing was as loud as his. My heart thudding just as hard and fast. His dick pulsed inside me, swelling and pushing against my inner walls. It felt like a second heartbeat, a separate, living creature that ebbed and flowed with each flex of my muscles. It was so strange to sweat and strain so hard without seemingly moving. Drenched in sweat, gasping for each ragged breath, I clenched down hard on him again, holding the squeeze, harder.

Until he broke.

His hips jerked beneath me, his arms flexing, pulling me harder against him as if he wanted to drag me inside his body. Hot semen flooded me, so much I could feel it filling me. It had nowhere else to go, not with his huge cock plugging me up. Or maybe that was the knot swelling up to lock us together. I wasn't sure what it actually looked like but it certainly felt like a grapefruit pressed against my cervix. Or maybe a watermelon. My abdomen even felt distended though maybe that was all in my head.

It didn't hurt. Exactly. Though the slightest bit more pressure would probably make me yelp.

"You didn't come." Now it was his turn to sound aggrieved. "And now we're fucking locked."

Everything still hummed inside me, but I'd been focused so intently on the Kegels that I'd pushed my own orgasm off. Or rather up higher, an impossible climb. I hovered at the edge of a cliff so high that I was actually afraid. If I went over the edge… I might not ever come back. "I'm… right… there. Just…"

"Then it's my turn to do a little experimentation." His chest expanded deeply, a massive bellows filling with air that humped my back and shoulders. As he exhaled, he let out a rattle like the amusement sound only deeper. A vibrating whirr that shimmered through his body into mine. Everywhere we touched. Even—especially—his dick.

Despite the sweat, goosebumps flared down my arms. My heart stuttered in my chest. But I still didn't come. I hovered right there, poised at the edge, pebbles raining down all around me, but I didn't go over the cliff.

"Angle's not quite right," he murmured. Cupping my buttocks in both hands, he pulled my lower body away from his slightly. Just enough to shift my body weight forward. The hard ridge of his cock pressed against my clit, sending sparks through my bloodstream. "Let's try that again."

The deep bellows heaved beneath me. The vicious rattle that made me instinctually quiver with the dread of a prey animal. And the bone-deep vibration that rolled through him. Directly to my clit.

That's what it felt like, at least. As if he'd focused a thousand-watt vibrator directly on my clit. I jerked and thrashed, my arms and legs twitching. Screaming, gasping, crying, I couldn't even hold on to him. I couldn't coordinate my muscles. Hold my head up. Breathe. All I could do was twitch in the onslaught of a vicious climax that tore through me. Rolling me down into darkness.

When did I get on a boat?

The thought didn't make sense. It took me several more breaths to remember who I was. Where I was.

The jungle. Lost. Chased.

The incredibly sexy man who'd found me. His gigantic body beneath me, his breath rocking me gently. His hands in my hair, on my back. I tried to lift my head but could only manage to roll my cheek slightly across his chest.

"There's my baby," he whispered, his voice a deep, low rumble. "I think it's safe to declare both experiments a success."

I laughed out a groan. "Only if your goal was to blast me to unconsciousness."

His fingers stroked over my face, his thumb rubbing along my lip and chin. "My goal is to blast you with pleasure every single time I touch you."

My muscles felt floppy but I finally managed to coordinate my elbow to brace against his chest so I could prop my face up. I drank in the casual sprawl of his body. Broad shoulders leaned against the flimsy cabin wall, his massive body completely filling up the tiny bed. It wouldn't surprise me if his feet hung off the other end, though I couldn't muster the strength to look.

I wasn't sure how much time had passed. I shifted slightly, sending a fresh wave of tingles cascading through my groin. He was still inside me, though it didn't feel like he was stuck. Just so damned big that he could casually lie with me in his arms and keep his dick inside me indefinitely.

Huffing out a laugh, I shook my head a little. Shell shocked and blissed out at the same time.

He cupped my cheek. "What are you thinking?"

"How long have I known you?"

"I found you at 20:49:16 yesterday, which means you have known me for almost eighteen and a half hours."

I blinked, trying to comprehend the fact that I hadn't even known him a full twenty-four hours yet. And we'd already had sex twice. Three times, actually, because we'd quickly gone for round two. Not counting the two climaxes I'd had just thinking about him.

But it was more than sex. Already.

It was the gentle way he stroked me constantly, as if he couldn't stop reveling in the simple texture of my hair or skin. Or he simply wanted that physical connection with me. And honestly, it was the same for me too. I wanted his scent in my nose, the heated velvet of his muscles against my face. I wanted to learn more of the unusual sounds he made and what they meant. All the little things he did that made me feel cherished.

Granted, the bar had been pretty fucking low from my past relationships. Just in the bedroom category he'd blown them all away, let alone how tender he was. How carefully he handled me despite his size.

But—and it was a HUGE one—I couldn't forget the monster that had chased me.

He was a freaking alien dinosaur soldier with technology that I couldn't even begin to understand.

Maybe he was right, and I was biologically compatible with him. What did that mean for our future? Could he stay on Earth? How would we live? What about the other aliens? Was anyone looking for me? Had they realized that I was lost yet?

How can I possibly go back to my old life after this?
Without him?

I couldn't even talk to anyone I knew. No one would believe me.

"Do not worry for the future, Natalie." His voice lowered even more, a deep rumbly bass that made my eyelids heavy and soothed the worry from my body. "I'm here now, and I'm not fucking going anywhere."

14

KROKTL

Lying with my mate in my arms was a treasure that I'd never even imagined would be mine. I'd lived with the squad my entire life. We were raised together. Trained together.

We killed together, and someday we'd die together.

So I'd always thought—until Axxol tore the squad apart and disappeared, stranding us on this backward planet.

The idea of me ever having my own mate was as foreign to me as the idea of splitting up the squad. Now both impossible things had happened, and nothing would ever be the same.

I wasn't trained for the possibility of being alone on an alien planet, because it never should have happened. My skills were the best in the universe—but they were limited. I had no idea what foods my human mate could eat. I couldn't make a jump off planet to somewhere safer. If she was injured or ill, I had no idea how to heal her. I could see the inner workings of her anatomy, but without a medic's training, I could do more damage than good if I tried to intervene in her body.

Worse, I had no solid plan for how I'd provide for her beyond this flimsy shack in the jungle. She needed solid, impenetrable walls. Soft bedding and plentiful food. Clothing to keep her warm and protected.

And if I were going to be her sole protection, I needed weapons. Lots of weapons. I needed to find a place of safety where I could stash her in comfort while I made sure to keep our nest secure. If she bore my young…

How could I possibly do everything alone to keep her safe, when I was programmed and bred to only be twenty percent of a team?

My beast paced vigorously inside me, slashing with teeth and claws. Furious anxiety wound me tighter and tighter, all my senses screaming with alarm. This place wasn't safe. Human smugglers were nearby. The people she'd been with might come searching for her. I had no idea how far away the rest of my squad might be, let alone if HQ had sent another squad to locate—exterminate—us.

I needed information. The sort of intel only another dynos could provide.

Too fucking risky. Gnashing my teeth, I tried to think of another alternative. If I tapped the grid, they'd know exactly where I was in seconds. If they were close…

But I'd know where they were too. I'd know if anyone else had been sighted. Maybe they'd managed to kill Axxol and were trying to find me. Though to what end, I couldn't begin to guess. Without our pilot, we'd still be trapped here. Unless another squad had joined us. Even then, we'd go straight to Nyan.

And I'd never see Natalie again.

Instinctively, I curled around her sleeping body, tightening my grip on her. She whimpered softly, so I quickly loosened my arms. But couldn't calm the beast roaring inside me. If I went back to HQ, they'd never let me keep a mate. If she were truly compatible for breeding, they'd...

Panting, I pushed the thought away. I couldn't even allow myself to contemplate what would happen if Dynosauros found us, or she'd wake up to the monstrous lizard that terrified her. I wouldn't survive without her, but I couldn't guarantee that my human mate had the same biological limitations. She might endure even if something happened to me.

My best bet was to use my skills. Run the point. Circle the squad—which was now solely my mate. In a typical mission, I easily covered four times as much ground as the rest of the squad, making loops back and forth, ahead and behind to see if we were going to encounter a target or if we were being followed. No one could cover as much ground as me in as short a time. Though running point meant I had to leave her.

Unprotected. Alone.

Not good. At all. I certainly couldn't leave her sleeping and unaware. I checked her vitals, measuring her brain waves and heart rate. Delta waves had increased, so she wasn't quite as deeply asleep, and her blood pressure had risen slightly. I began to stroke her back and arm, a soft, light touch that gradually deepened in pressure.

"Natalie," I whispered. "I need you to wake up, baby."

She blinked languorously and nuzzled deeper against my chest. "But you're so warm."

"Mmmm, and you're so soft and tasty. But I'd like to check our perimeter and scout for a safer place."

She tipped her head back, her brow furrowed with concern. "Have you heard something?"

"No, not yet. But I'd like to find a more secure location with easy access to food and weapons."

Her eyes widened, her heart rate quickening, but she nodded and began untangling our limbs. I'd been the one to wake her, but I still regretted losing the feel of her soft thigh pressed between mine. "I'd like to know if anyone from base camp is looking for me yet."

I pushed up out of the bed and grabbed the small handgun I'd found taped underneath the kitchen counter when I claimed the place. "Do you know how to use this?"

She shook her head. "No. I've never even held a gun before."

"This one's easy." I pressed it into her hand, holding my fingers around hers until she adjusted her grip. "Move this slide back, point, and pull the trigger. It's already loaded."

"Wow, it's heavy. I'm assuming it'll have a pretty big kick if I have to use it?"

"It has a recoil, yes. The trigger is sensitive enough that you can deliver several shots quickly without having to release it. There are eighteen rounds but they'll go quickly. I haven't located additional ammunition for this weapon yet, or I'd have you practice."

She pushed it back toward me though I didn't take the gun from her. "You should have it, then. I don't know anything about how to use it."

Slowly I shook my head, letting the beast peek out from behind my eyes. "I'm your primary weapon. This gun is just to use if I'm away scouting. But trust me—if you shout my name, I'll hear you from miles away. I'll scorch the earth getting to you and slaughter anything and anyone in my path. This gun will just give you a little more security until I can reach you."

Her bottom lip wobbled. "It's bad, isn't it?"

Gently, I took the gun from her and laid it back on the counter in plain sight. Then I cupped her cheeks in both hands and leaned down to press a kiss to her forehead. "I haven't scouted for a few hours, so I don't honestly know yet. No one was anywhere near us then. I just need to be sure, and I don't like to leave you unprotected. I'll feel better once I get us to a safer location."

"Where?" she whispered.

"I don't know yet," I admitted, hating my own limitations. "Away from humans first. Then I'll worry about other dyni."

"Or those killer ones?"

I kissed the tip of her nose. "Don't worry about them yet. Let's tackle the threats one by one, yeah? So humans first. I'm going to make sure the smugglers left the area. If you need to call someone to let them know you're alright, do so. I trust you, baby. Tell them whatever you need to if you have someone who may worry."

She shook her head. "Only my friend, Holly. I might let her know that I'm alright so they can call off any search parties that might be trying to find me."

Her stomach rumbled, making my eyes narrow with concern. Her blood sugar smelled low again. "Eat another banana. I'll scout the smugglers first since they had weapons, and then I'll procure more supplies from the village. I won't be long."

I strode to the door but paused, looking back at her one last time. My little human mate smiled bravely at me. "No beans this time."

"I'll see what I can do."

15

NATALIE

I stood frozen a moment like a deer in headlights. Nervous energy pumped through my veins but there wasn't a whole lot I could do. I didn't have to pack up a tent or grab my things. He'd already done that. The clothes I'd been wearing yesterday were destroyed. I didn't think I had time for another shower, though I'm sure that I could probably use one. My nose had evidently adjusted to my stench.

Or rather, *his* stench. Though if I stopped and thought about that too long, I knew what would happen.

Grabbing my larger duffle bag that Kroktl had retrieved from camp, I pulled out fresh clothes, deodorant, and a brush. My hair was a mess, but I did a quick tidy and pulled it back into a ponytail. Dragging on clean shorts, I paused a moment, studying my legs and ankles. No scratches. Even after running through all kinds of underbrush yesterday. Even weirder, no bruises or scrapes on my knee, even though I clearly remembered falling.

My joints and muscles were still sore, but not from falling. At least I wouldn't get a nasty infection, but unease niggled. It hadn't even been twenty-four hours yet. I wasn't a fast healer. Had being with him done something to my DNA? Had he healed me? But when?

At least I felt a little more like myself once I was back in real clothes. Natalie Whit, graduate student from Crystal Springs, Texas.

Not the alien dinosaur's sex babe. Though that had a nice ring to it.

Snorting at myself, I quickly went through all the things he'd brought from camp, thinking I might need to discard some things or repack it. But he'd done an excellent job making it all tidy. I held the coffee cup he'd accidentally stolen, weighing whether I should leave it behind, but I decided to keep it. It might be useful until we got to a new place. A safer place.

Which made my jittery energy skyrocket even higher. I needed to *do* something. Something productive. I glanced around the shack but I had no idea what was his versus what had been left behind by the previous owner. I didn't want him wasting time shredding up a bunch of old clothes that smelled like another man.

With a sigh, I grabbed my phone and flopped back down on the bed.

Three missed calls, all from Holly's number. Oh no. I'd forgotten all about her, stuck with Dr. Sleezeball. I clicked on her number.

"Nat? Thank god you're alright! Where are you?"

"Sorry, I'm fine. I didn't hear my phone. Are you okay?"

"Dr. Snyder is pissed. He got a call last night about some issues, and then again first thing this morning that you were missing. What happened?"

Hesitating, I tried to decide how much to tell her. I liked Holly well enough but I wouldn't exactly call her a friend. We were acquaintances. We got along in class but hadn't really done much work together until this trip. We'd linked arms metaphorically to endure Snyder's skeevy vibes but I didn't know much about her background.

Deciding to play it safe, I said, "Tomas and Jairo left me at the dig site. I tried to get back to camp on my own, but I got lost."

"Why didn't you call for help? Are you back to camp now?"

"I didn't have a signal. I found an abandoned hut to sleep for a few hours and noticed that you'd called. My phone's about dead." A lie—but she didn't have to know that. "I just wanted to let you know I was okay."

"But you're not back at camp?" She repeated slowly. "With Snyder?"

"No. I haven't seen him. I'm still out in the jungle somewhere."

Silence hung between us, and it dawned on me that maybe she was going through the same mental gymnastics as me. Could she trust me? She didn't know me either.

"Something happened last night," she finally said. "He was angry but tried to play it off as no big deal. At least it kept him from trying any funny business with me."

"I was worried about you being alone with him."

"Yeah. Me too. But he ended up on his phone most of the night. I could hear him talking through the wall." Another long pause. "Then the news this morning that you were gone really set him off."

Not for one minute did I even consider that he cared about my wellbeing. "Let me guess—he thinks whatever went down is my fault."

"What happened last night? Other than you getting lost?"

She sounded doubtful, as if she didn't believe me. Which

honestly, made me proud of my abilities. All of the research about the location of the dig site was mine, so it was suspicious that I'd get lost—when I'd led everyone to that exact spot in the first place.

"I started back to camp alone, and at first, everything was fine. It got dark, which was pretty scary, but I still thought I'd be okay. But then I heard something. Like an animal. A big animal. It chased me off the path. I ran, got turned around, fell in a hole, and finally found a place to hide."

"You didn't see anyone else?"

Why would she ask, unless she knew about Kroktl? But how could she? If I told her I'd found a naked man in the jungle who claimed to be an alien… Oh wait. There had been someone else last night. "I didn't see anyone, but I heard some men shouting in the distance. They sounded… unfriendly. I didn't want to risk calling them for help when they were yelling at each other."

"They could have been the search party."

"No one knew I was missing yet," I reminded her. "Plus no one was shouting my name. They were yelling in Spanish, but I couldn't really understand it. They were talking too fast and too far away."

"I don't know, Nat. Something weird is going on. I've never seen Snyder so… so… paranoid. Angry. Like punch a wall angry. I'm worried what he'll do when they find you."

I tried to think of a way to tell her the truth—without betraying anything about Kroktl. "I'm not planning on going back to camp."

"What? How are you getting out of the jungle then? Let alone home. Snyder is already pissed. He'll make your life miserable once we get back on campus. I don't know about you, but I don't have any money to get home by myself."

"I can't explain everything now. I'm okay. Don't worry about me."

"Tell me, Natalie." Her voice sharpened. "What the fuck is going on?"

"I… I met someone."

She snorted. "Yeah, sure. You just happened to run into a hot guy in the jungle who swept you off your feet and gave you a night of so much pleasure that you're abandoning your career plans and entire future for him."

I couldn't help but smile. "Yeah, pretty much."

"Wait a fucking minute. You've got to be teasing me. Right? Shit like that doesn't happen. Did you hit your head when you fell in that hole?"

I heard a noise outside. Footsteps. Oh shit. It sounded like boots.

I never heard Kroktl when he was approaching. He certainly didn't wear boots.

Clutching the phone against my ear, I scrambled off the bed, staying low to the ground. I reached up and grabbed the gun off the counter. "Someone's here."

"Who? Mr. Hot Guy?"

"No," I whispered, crouching down behind the tiny counter.

"Rescue team?"

Hands shaking, I ran through Kroktl's instructions on how to use the gun. "They're not calling my name."

Only eighteen bullets. Did I risk firing them all of now? Before he was back? If I saved the bullets for later but died, I'd be pretty fucking pissed at myself.

Someone called out further away. Male. The person I'd heard close by yelled back something about *choza*. Hut.

"What were the men doing in the jungle last night?" I whispered to Holly. "And why would that make Snyder mad?"

"I think they're smugglers," she replied in a rush. "He kept talking about money and trouble."

That rang a bell. Kroktl had said that this area was known for drug smugglers. I flipped the safety switch. "They're here."

16

NATALIE

Heart pounding, I stared at the door, the gun held between both my hands, close to my chest. I'd set the phone down on the counter, still connected to Holly. At least there'd be a witness of whatever happened, though I didn't think it would make much of a difference. What could a lone American college student do?

The door thumped open, making me flinch. A man stood in the doorway. I couldn't see his face, but he was dressed in camo and held a big fucking rifle casually in his hand. I didn't recognize him from camp, but he could be part of a rescue party.

Keeping myself as small and still as possible, I watched as he glanced around the dingy hut. His gaze narrowed in on my backpack on the bed. He yelled over his shoulder, "¡Más acá!" and adjusted the rifle forward.

Ready to shoot.

Bracing myself, I pulled the trigger. Several shots fired, too rapidly for my brain to even count them. My shoulders and arms jerked with the recoil. Too low. I got him in the thigh. He bellowed and jumped back out of the doorway.

Everything slowed. Or maybe my mind had slipped into super-sonic mode. More men yelled outside, calling back and forth to the man I'd shot. At least a handful of men. I didn't have enough bullets to hold them all off. Especially when they were armed better than me.

Kroktl wouldn't be too far away. He might have already heard the gunfire and be headed back. He'd sworn he'd come like a glaze of light if he heard me call for him. How long would it take, though? If all these men had rifles, they'd blast this hut to smithereens before he could help. I certainly couldn't hold them off with a handgun.

I had to play this smart. Win the long game. Give him time to arrive.

"Go away!" I yelled. "Or I'll shoot again!"

A different man called back. "We don't want to hurt you, Natalie Whit."

I clenched the gun so hard that my fingers ached. They knew my name. So they had to be working for Snyder.

"You're lost, sí? I'm sorry that we frightened you. We're here to help."

Yeah right. Rescue teams didn't carry AR-15s or whatever rifles those were. But if they thought I was naïve and stupid, they wouldn't kill me. At least right away. "You're from camp?" I asked, letting my voice quiver.

"Your professor sent us to find you." A man slowly approached the open doorway, his hands held out on either side. He didn't have a gun that I could see. "We should have called out to you, Natalie. We've been looking for you all morning. Put the gun down so no one else gets hurt."

I sniffled loudly. "Okay. Please don't hurt me. I just want to go home."

"Sí, sí. Come along now and be a good girl."

Inwardly, I shuddered. I didn't like the sinister undertones in that phrase at all. As if he was already planning all the ways he was going to hurt me before we got back to camp.

The man I'd shot growled something low and vicious, biting off his words on a groan. I couldn't suppress a quick grin. At least I'd wounded one of them.

"Come out now and no one else gets hurt," the second man said.

I pushed up to my feet, forcing my shaking legs to carry me toward the door. I held my phone in one hand and the gun in the other, away from my body. *I just have to survive until Kroktl gets here. Whatever that takes.* "I'm coming out."

The soldier quickly snagged the gun from me and jerked his head at a third man. He took my phone and then brushed past me into the hut. Three more men stood ten or twenty paces away, guns ready. The man I'd shot leaned against the wall of the hut, while another soldier wrapped a bandage around his thigh.

"Who are you?" I asked the man who'd been speaking. I assumed he was the leader of this little group. "Who do you work for?"

He flashed a tight, small smile as he tucked my gun into his waistband. "I could ask the same of you, chica."

The man came out of the hut with my bags slung over his shoulder. They spoke rapidly in Spanish, and though I tried to listen and translate, I just couldn't keep up. I scanned the trees and bushes around the hut, looking for Kroktl. Surely he'd heard the gun. I wanted to shout for him, but I didn't want to set these assholes off, either. So far, they hadn't hurt me, though the man I'd shot was definitely glaring at me murderously.

"Where's your friend?" The leader asked.

Startled, I tried to play it off with confusion. "My friend? Do you mean Holly?"

"You must think we're pretty stupid. Who are you working for?"

"Dr. Snyder. I work with him—"

Something slammed into the side of my head so hard it was like a thick black curtain dropped over my eyes. I felt my body slumping, slowly falling, and all I could think about was trying to call for help. *"Kroktl!"*

KROKTL

My whole world exploded in a raging ball of fury.

Blood. I smelled my mate's blood on the air.

Someone. Had FUCKING TOUCHED. My. Fucking. MATE.

Nose high, I tasted the air, focusing on the sweet flavor of her blood that shouldn't be there. I smelled humans. At least five or six. I screamed out a battle cry that silenced the jungle in a five-mile radius.

Motherfuckers. Will. Die!

I tore through the jungle, following that tantalizing hint of her blood. It only took me a few minutes to realize the trail led back to her group's camp. One of her own people had hurt her? Taken her? I'd fucking end them for betraying her trust.

Breathing hard, I tried to get a grip on the beast's fury.

The last thing she'd want to see was her new lover ripping the limbs and heads off her supposed friends and eating them whole. Besides, I didn't want to be seen unless I had no other choice. The camp that'd been nearly empty a few hours ago now buzzed with jeeps and people. Soldiers. Would they use armed men for a rescue mission?

We would, but I didn't know much about human military tactics. Crouched in good cover, I scanned all the vehicles and tents, taking an assessment of their weaponry. Rifles. Nothing heavy. Nothing up to penetrating my armored hide.

I found the tent where she lay. They'd tied her arms behind her back. A large contusion swelled on her left temple. I'd have to monitor it and make sure she didn't experience a brain bleed.

Fucking hell. I might have to contact Snryx. If she needed anything more than basic medical assistance, I wouldn't have a choice. I'd do anything to save her.

Even if it cost me my life.

17

NATALIE

Groggy and fuzzy, I woke up in my tent. My head ached like I had a bad hangover. Had Tomas brought out the mystery jug again? I'd learned my lesson the first night. I didn't remember drinking.

Blinking bleary eyes, I tried to remember. I didn't think I should be here, though this was definitely my tent. The same scent of mildew. The familiar watermark stain down the side that looked like a face. There was its eye. Strong, full lips. Hint of hair curling along the neck. No, that wasn't quite right. Leaves. Not hair.

Kroktl didn't have hair.

I jolted wide awake. Everything came pouring back. The men coming to the hut. One of them must have hit me. Had I managed to call Kroktl before I passed out? I couldn't remember.

I couldn't move. My hands were numb, my arms heavy. It took me a moment to understand why. My hands were tied behind my back. It took me forever to roll up on one side and heave myself upright, wincing at the pain in my head.

"Kroktl," I rasped out, choking on my dry mouth. My

tongue felt like a wad of cotton. No way he heard that, but I couldn't get any louder until I had a drink of water.

What if he thought I'd run from him? Abandoned him?

I was back here at camp. Would he even think to come here and look for me? Sure, he claimed he'd be able to follow my scent, but if he came here and saw me back with my people, he might assume that I'd come here willingly.

"Stop it," I told myself firmly. *"Stop panicking."*

He would find me. With his super-soldier senses, he'd know that I was hurt or at least held against my will. He'd take one look at the goose egg that was probably swollen on my forehead and know exactly what had happened.

He's not going to leave me here.

"Ah," Dr. Snyder said as he ducked into the tent. "You're awake. Good. I was worried about you."

"Yeah right," I muttered.

Old Natalie would have bitten her tongue, afraid of ruining her future career. New Natalie didn't give a rat's ass what this asshole thought. I didn't have any proof, but I sure had my suspicions about what had upset him last night, and it had nothing to do with me getting lost in the jungle.

He sat down on the camp stool beside the cot with a heavy sigh, as if I'd just failed his final exam. Twirling his favorite wanna-be Indiana Jones hat, he couldn't even meet my gaze. "Well, Miss Whit, you've certainly caused me a considerable amount of trouble."

I didn't even try to stifle a sarcastic laugh. *Good.* "How's that?"

His eyes narrowed at my attitude. "I had to hire people to find you and skipped out on several important meetings to make sure you were found."

Bullshit. Those men with guns hadn't been on a rescue mission. "Ah, yes, those very important people you were wining and dining at the hotel. I'm sure they couldn't find out that the twenty-six-year-old female grad student——that you'd left in the jungle alone with two strangers—was missing."

"Tomas came highly recommended as a local guide. He wasn't supposed to leave you like that."

I snorted. "Yeah, well, babies can fuck up the best-laid plans. It's not Tomas's fault he had an emergency."

His eyes flared at my language. I'd always taken great pains to be the ideal student. Not too coarse, not too loud, not too brash. Amiable without too many opinions. Always *"yes sir,"* and *"could I help you with that, sir?"*

Complete bullshit. I just wished that it hadn't taken me all these years to figure out that swallowing down my pride and anger at the unfairness of it all was a losing battle. It'd taken almost losing my life in the jungle to realize that none of it mattered. If I had to pretend to be his trained monkey to get a position at the university, then I'd be miserable. Forever. I'd always be tainted by that subordinate association, at least in my own eyes and heart. And honestly, that was all that mattered.

"It seems as though you've wandered far afield from the young woman that I thought you were, along with leaving our safe and secure camp location."

Watching his reaction, I shrugged casually. "So you mean I wasn't supposed to see those men in the jungle last night? How shocking."

His hand twitched on his hat so hard that he dented the perfect brim.

"Now I'm Miss Whit instead of sweetie," I drawled. "Why? Because you suddenly realize I have a brain in my head and have seen through your disguise?"

"I have no idea what you're talking about."

I rolled my shoulders, shifting uncomfortably to remind him that my hands were still tied behind my back. "The grad student gets left in a deserted Maya ruin overnight in the middle of a protected park with limited civilization. When she's finally found and identified, she's treated like a prisoner. The only thing that makes sense is that I saw too much. Those smugglers were yours. That's why you make so many trips down here, right? You bring along a good little assistant to do the work for appearances, and then you go off to make your drug deals. It must have been a pretty sweet deal for you. You've been making these so-called archeology trips for years, conning hopeful and desperate students to do your research for you while you make a hefty sum on the side."

The perfectly charming facade cracked a little. "There's always twenty or more silly girls standing in line to join the next dig. Pretty ones, and smart ones. You know which one you are."

That comment might have hurt me a few days ago. But I'd experienced a lifetime of adventure in just twenty-four hours. I'd finally experienced real passion. The kind of passion that would make a person burn up the world to have again.

With a slow smile, I lowered my lashes and gave him a sultry look. I almost chuckled out loud at the way his eyes widened with surprise. "Yeah. I'm both."

His gaze dropped down to my chest as if he'd only just realized that I had breasts. Unfortunately, I hadn't bothered with a bra, and the T-shirt was thin. It gave me the creeps to know he was ogling me.

"Our men were attacked last night," he finally said, though he wasn't able to drag his gaze back up to my face. "You wouldn't know anything about that, would you, now, Miss Whit?"

Voices rose outside and one of the armed men poked his head inside. I hadn't caught his name, but he was the man I'd assumed to be the leader when they found the hut. "Trouble."

Dr. Snyder stood but still stared at me with a pole-axed look on his face. "What kind of trouble?"

"Two of my men are gone."

Finally, Snyder turned away, and I drooped with relief. To think that I'd once found the man attractive—before I'd seen the douchebag in action.

Someone yelled outside. Gunfire. Both men crowded at the tent flap, trying to see what was going on. The soldier pressed a phone to his ear.

"What is it?" Dr. Snyder asked.

"Another man's gone. They saw some kind of… animal. They're pursuing it now."

The way he said animal made me smile. Lizard. Monster.

Kroktl's here, and he's pissed.

Or rather, his creature was here. I shivered, relieved but also terrified. He said he was in control of his beast. It would remember me.

Right?

His words replayed in my head on repeat. *Whatever you do, don't run.*

18

NATALIE

"I want out of here." Dr. Snyder suddenly didn't sound like his movie hero. Unless it was Indy facing a big pit of snakes.

The soldier didn't look at him but gave a short nod. "Figured you'd want out of this so you could wash your hands of whatever went down. Leave the girl. I'll take care of her."

I flinched. I knew too much, and I didn't have to be an action-movie star to realize what that meant.

Dr. Snyder gave me an uncomfortable look over his shoulder, not quite able to meet my eyes, but not happy either. "I don't like it."

It almost made me feel a little better about him in general… until he shrugged apologetically and left the tent. Asshole to the end.

I yelled after him. "Coward!"

"You've got two choices." Camo-man still scanned outside, using the scope on his gun. "I can shoot you now, here, nice and clean. Or you can take your chances in the jungle. Nice American girl lost in the jungle is easier to sell than white girl found shot in camp as far as I'm concerned, but you're a long way from home. No one's going to care much anyway."

"I'll take my chances."

He barked out a laugh and glanced at me with a glint of respect in his eyes. "I'll free your hands, chica. You should at least have a sporting chance."

Moving closer, I turned around, waiting for him to free me. Pins and needles burned in my fingers and up my wrists as he untied me. I shook my hands out and lifted my arms slowly, wincing as the burning intensified. I didn't think I'd been out that long, but my shoulders and arms complained at every small movement. "Do you work for the Guatemalan government?"

He returned to watching out the tent flap. "I work for whoever pays me. Get whatever you're taking and let's go."

I scooped up my backpack, but I didn't bother with the duffle bag. I didn't know how far I'd have to hike, assuming I made it out of camp in one piece. "Do you know what's out there?"

"There are many things out there that will kill you."

A terrible roar made Camo-man jerk up the rifle before him, ready to shoot. "We don't want to get trapped in here. Not enough visibility. I need to see it to shoot, so let's go."

As soon as I ducked outside the tent, all hell broke loose. A small group of soldiers stood together, shooting into the trees. They were mowing down limbs and sending up geysers of bark and dirt. A wave of panic rocked through me. What if they actually managed to wound Kroktl? Could he be hurt? Facing the jungle to find him was easy. Facing it without him...

Another roar rumbled the ground. He was still alive. Hopefully unhurt. But could he take care of this many soldiers? All armed to the teeth and shooting at everything that moved? I looked around wildly, trying to find him. If I fled into the jungle, the men would probably accidentally shoot me trying to get him. Plus, the no running thing.

Camo-man took my arm, tugging me along with him. Trying to buy some time, I went with him. His own men wouldn't shoot him. Probably. Right? So I was safer with him, at least temporarily, giving Kroktl time to eliminate more of the panicked shooters.

Dr. Snyder ran back toward us, pale and eyes wild. "Get me on the helicopter."

"Double," Camo-man replied calmly.

"Done."

He took the lead, letting go of my arm. We ran behind the larger communal tent and ducked down at the corner. Camo-man scanned the area and then ran for the next tent. One minute he was almost to the tent, safe, turning back to wave us across, and the next, the jungle swallowed him. It happened so fast, it was like a magic trick. He didn't even scream or get a shot off.

"Fuck," Dr. Snyder whispered, his voice shaking.

I searched the trees, trying to find the same monster-shape I'd seen last night so I could run toward him. Correction: walk with great purpose.

Something tall and wide, like a giraffe or grizzly standing up on its hind legs... Glowing red eyes. But I couldn't see anything through the thick brush. I couldn't smell his musky scent either, so I wasn't sure which way to go.

Three soldiers joined us. One with a bandage on his leg. Great. He leveled his gun at me and motioned me toward Dr. Snyder. Though from the dark look in the soldier's eyes, he really hoped that I would ignore his order so he could shoot me.

"This way." Dr. Snyder darted back inside the loose circle of tents, avoiding the darker shadows on the edge of camp.

"Slow down!" I told him. "You don't run from predators."

Not that he would listen. The wounded soldier shoved me in the back so hard that I flew forward, struggling to stay on my feet. I tripped over something and went down. I saw stars again. My head throbbed with every beat of my heart, and I couldn't focus my eyes. I couldn't seem to coordinate my body. To get up. Stand. Walk.

Don't run.

The soldier reached down and hauled me up by my arm, his grip vicious. Blinking furiously, I stared at the thing I'd tripped over. A lumpy sack. Stained in red. A sack of meat?

No. A body.

Horrifically fascinated, I couldn't look away. The head and shoulders were mostly gone, leaving a midsection that looked like a sack rather than a once-living body. One boot was gone, along with most of the lower leg.

Kroktl had done that. His creature. He'd ripped a man apart like he was just a side of meat.

I hoped he did the same to this asshole dragging me along.

Everyone was shouting, or bombs were going off. Clamor in my head. Dizzy and sick, I couldn't get my feet to work together. Snyder came back and grabbed my other arm, jerking on my shoulder, his mouth moving. But I couldn't hear his words over the thunderous din in my head.

Something brushed against me. Turning my head, I watched the scene unfold like a slow-motion movie. A dark shape. Scales. So close that I could see the pattern. Mottled dark green and black with specs of bright red like blood. Red Raptor Rex. A tail slithered by, thick and long, very much like an alligator. Someone screamed. Teeth crunched. I heard the splinter of bones like gravel crunching underfoot. Hot, wet blood splattered my face.

The creature. Kroktl. I tried to reconcile the man I'd fucked all night and this beast. He was so much bigger than

I'd thought. Huge. Towering over the soldiers. Legs hung out of his mouth. One was bandaged. Still kicking. The monster pinned another man to the ground with one massive hind leg, digging claws into the soldier's abdomen. I remembered how long those claws were. How sharp.

The soldier screamed and kicked, tangled up in his own intestines. The monster's tail slashed hard to the side, catching the other soldier in the face. His head exploded. It was like an Internet video of a watermelon blowing up. Only with teeth and scales and claws coated in blood and brains and guts.

I swayed. Unable to look away. Unable to move.

Someone jerked on my arm. Heaved me over a shoulder. Jolting my throbbing head so much it was all I could do not to throw up. A gray haze settled over me like cobwebs. Distantly, I realized that I was sliding into shock, but I didn't know what to do to stop it. I couldn't think with my head splitting open.

Dumped down on the ground like a sack of potatoes. Not the ground—something hard. Metal. Snyder climbed up beside me. Whirring sounds, wind rushing around. The ground started to move away.

Helicopter. He'd asked the man to get him to the helicopter.

Oh my god. Someone was trying to pull me up off the floor. Belt me into a harness.

Trap me. Carry me away from Kroktl.

I could see him now in all his monstrous glory. Red eyes burning, he glared up at the helicopter. Huge mouth gaping open with impossibly huge teeth. Thick, powerful thighs. Vicious talons raking the ground. He crouched and exploded upward, razor claws extending. So close, I could almost smell his scent. I stared into those awful eyes and tried to see the man.

Not the monster. Not the creature that'd turned a person into a meat sack. Or pulled out a man's intestines or bit another soldier in half.

He landed hard, shaking the ground. Jostling the torn apart bodies that littered the ground all around him. Dead. They were all dead. Every man who hadn't made it to the helicopter. Ten? Twenty? I wasn't sure.

Throwing his head back he bellowed so loudly that I could hear it even over the helicopter's blades. Fury and agony, he screamed, tail lashing, claws raking the ground. I could almost hear his voice in my head. *I'll find you. I'll follow you.*

He stilled. Lowered his head. His tail curled up around his legs.

Shame? Acceptance? Sacrifice?

I wasn't sure. But all the fight seemed to go out of him. Maybe he thought I'd be better off without him. Or worse, maybe he thought I *wanted* to get away. Maybe he thought I was so scared of his creature that I'd rather be on this helicopter with the sleezy professor who'd been secretly working with drug smugglers than stay behind with a horrible creature like him.

My vision blurred again, but this time it was tears. I couldn't bear the thought of him being alone. Convinced that I'd fled him. That I feared him. Especially after all the care he'd shown me already.

In one night, he'd given me more passion and care than any man in my entire life. Granted, the bar was on the ground in that regard. The men I knew were all trash. But he'd done his best to give me a choice, even when his own instincts drove him to mate. Yes, my human brain still cringed at that word. I didn't know what the future held with an alien creature like him.

His life was dangerous. Complex in ways I couldn't even

comprehend. He had enemies in his own squad, trapped on a planet that was just as alien to him as he was to me. Yet no one had ever touched me with more tenderness and devotion in my entire life.

Before I could tell myself that I was crazy, I moved closer to the door, gripping the metal frame for dear life. How fast were we flying? How far away was the ground? It looked like twenty feet or more. But it didn't matter.

He was down there.

"Kroktl!"

He jerked his head up, red eyes locked on me. Leaping into a dead run, he quickly caught up, keeping pace with the helicopter. My stomach quivered. The fall was probably going to kill me, but I could almost hear his voice in my head.

I got you.

Closing my eyes, I jumped.

19

KROKTL

She jumped. My fucking badass mate fucking *jumped* out of a moving helicopter like it was no big deal.

I knew without a doubt that I could catch her. That wasn't a problem.

What filled me with sheer terror was the thought that I might accidentally bite her in half when I did.

I leaped as high as possible to reduce her time in the air, but it was still a hell of a fall. Opening my jaws wide, I snagged her around the waist. Air whomped out of her lungs at the impact, but she didn't scream. Though she didn't move, either. Probably scared to death.

Please, please be alright!

I landed, letting my legs take the impact like coiled springs. With a tip of my head, I spilled her down in front of me, using my forearms to control her tumble to the ground and hopefully keep my teeth out of her fragile skin.

The helicopter whirled back around. Bullets tore across the ground straight at us. I dropped to a crouch over the top of her, taking a few nicks in my hide, but nothing serious. Only armor-piercing rounds would have a prayer against my scales, and even that wouldn't stop me unless they managed a direct hit in my heart or skull. Still, I didn't like being out in the open like this. I couldn't afford to be documented or noticed by any planetary authority. With an off-grid squad deployed, HQ would be monitoring Earth's communications. If a picture got leaked of the prehistoric-looking creature in Guatemala, the jungles of South America would be crawling with dyni.

Assassins. Looking to put me down or bring me in.

Frustration and urgency burned in my gut. In this form, I couldn't tell Natalie that we needed to get the hell out of here. She'd already done the unthinkable by bailing out of a helicopter, but she wasn't safe yet. Not by a long shot. My attempts at communication before had only terrified her, even when I'd been as soothing as possible. She certainly hadn't wanted my help. Not in this form.

But I couldn't leave her either, not even to try and draw enemy fire. One stray bullet would end her fragile life. She didn't have my scaled hide for protection.

Her hands slid up my chest. She was touching me—and not freaking out. "I'm okay. Do what you need to do to get us out of here."

Hold on, baby. My muscles coiled, waiting for the helicopter to pass back overhead. Then I jerked her up against my chest, gripping her thighs to lock her in place. Her arms looped around my neck, squeezing tightly. Hanging in front of me, she jounced with each step, though she was strong enough to keep a good grip on my neck.

A quick sprint got us into the jungle. Under good cover, I crouched, letting her drop back to the ground to rest her arms. She swayed, her head dropping back against my chest as if she couldn't even hold it up. She didn't even mind touching my creature—which told me a lot about how out of it she was.

Worry made me hiss and growl with helpless rage. I didn't want to scare her, but her condition was definitely scaring the shit out of me. I smelled fresh blood, so I'd at least scratched her up some, but I didn't think I'd injured her internally. No, whatever ailed her had been dealt by the hands of those fucking humans who'd taken her from the hut.

The helicopter still whirled around, scanning the jungle. With my coloring, I'd be impossible to find if I chose to simply stay and hide, but I'd rather get her to safety. Not back to the hut. Not when humans had already infiltrated it. I needed a place of safety for her. A nest.

Mentally cursing this fucking miserable planet, I hefted her back up against my chest, cradling her as gently as possible. She couldn't hike, not in this condition, and I could move faster if I carried her. I had to hope that I wasn't mentally scarring her by keeping her so close to the monster. I couldn't risk shifting in front of her yet. That would really push her over the edge. Besides, I could cover more ground as dynos anyway. Distance from this place and the people who'd seen me would ease some of my concern.

I loped through the jungle, keeping my pace as even and smooth as possible. Away from the village I'd found earlier. It was too risky to take her anywhere near people. Deep wilderness would be best, though I had to worry about food and shelter for my human mate.

Not to mention medical care. Her body temperature was lower than it should be, and she shivered. In the humid warmth of a jungle. Not good. Not good at all.

I found a small stream of good clean water and a sandy, flat spot to rest. Steep rocky cliffs rose on either side of the stream, giving me a semblance of security, though I'd feel better with thick, solid walls around her. I found the sunniest patch of beach and lay her down so I could scan her body for injury.

First, I nosed up her shirt enough to look for injuries from when I'd caught her. She had a few scratches on her back, but no deep punctures. A fucking miracle. Her head was a problem, though. Swollen with an angry looking bruise, tender to the touch. She blinked repeatedly, as if she couldn't see well. Her pupils were wide and dark despite the sun. Her face was pale, her skin clammy.

I had no food. No shelter. No medical equipment. She still wore the backpack, though the other bag I'd fetched earlier was gone. I took the straps off her shoulders and searched for anything that might help her.

Yes. An empty water bottle in the side. I flipped the lid off and left her momentarily to get some water from the stream. When I returned, she'd managed to sit up, though she leaned forward, bracing her head on her knees. I let out a low, soft breath, a sigh more than anything, so I wouldn't alarm her.

Her head came up. Eyes wide, she stared at me a moment without moving.

I waited in place, keeping my body still, head low, lips carefully covering my teeth. Though I couldn't help but scan her continuously. Body temperature was still too low. Heart rate was slower than her basal rate. I blinked, switching to scan the deeper tissues in her brain. I didn't detect any fresh bleeding, though her brain waves were definitely off. Slower, as if she were drowsy or just waking up.

One corner of her lip quirked up. "How did you know?" She rasped, holding out her hand.

I passed the water to her, careful not to let a claw touch her. She drank several long swallows but then paused, her shoulders drooping, as if even drinking was too much effort. Her blood sugars were low again. I rummaged in the bag, looking for anything edible. A wrapped rectangle smelled organic, so I offered it to her.

Wincing, she shook her head. "My stomach's too queasy for chocolate right now."

Another red flag. Gently, I nudged the bottom of the water bottle, encouraging her to drink more. She took a few more swallows but had to rest again.

She studied me openly, without the same fear as when I first found her. Though I didn't think she was ready for me to shift in front of her. "You're definitely bigger. Wow. You're showing your T-rex side."

There was so much I wanted to say. I wanted to crush her against me with gratitude. Relief. Joy. Admiration. Adoration.

She'd jumped out of a helicopter with complete trust that I would catch her. Me. She trusted me. Just last night, she'd flinched away from me and ran as soon as I turned my back. Today, she'd touched me and even rested her head against me. She'd been in my mouth. Her entire body.

Ecstasy rolled through me at the memory of her skin on my tongue. Not that I wanted her to take such a risk again, but oh, the memory would replay in my mind every time I closed my eyes. The taste of her skin. The softness of her luscious body. The delicate scrape of my teeth on her tender abdomen. It was all I could do not to crank my jaws wide again and see if she'd take another jump on my tongue.

Crazy. Stupid.

She was alive. That's all I needed.

Though I wouldn't ever forget.

NATALIE

A monster crouched beside me. A creature that I'd seen tear men apart like they were toys and turn them into bloody chunks. That same creature crouched close beside me. Close enough to seize me in one big gulp.

Instead, all he did was remind me to take another drink of water.

I could still feel the leathery texture of his skin—hide—against my cheek. Distinct knobs of his scales. The rich, musky scent that had been so terrifyingly strange but now…

It made me feel safe. Because it meant that he was close.

Maybe it was shock, or the bump to the head, but I had the feeling it was the mating instinct he'd mentioned earlier, because I really wanted to cuddle against him. I wanted to show him that I wasn't afraid.

Because I wasn't. He'd held me in vicious teeth that I'd seen rip a man apart just moments before, and I didn't have a mark on me. Though would he welcome that kind of touch from me? Was it too… intimate? When he was in his monster form?

Shivers raced up my spine and my stomach wobbled around the water. I didn't feel good at all, and I just wanted comfort. His comfort. His protection. So fuck it.

I tipped forward, letting my entire body fall against him. Knowing that he would catch me.

Surprisingly dexterous claws—hands—pulled me up against his broad chest. He made several short coughs, his nose bumping against my shoulder. Worry vibrated through him, his heart pounding like a timpani drum against my ear. "I'm okay. Just hold me. Please? I'm so tired. I just want to rest."

He nudged me again with his snout, until I turned my head and looked into his nearest eye. He blinked, circles flaring in the glowing red orb. I wasn't sure what he was looking at.

The tip of his tongue touched the knot on my head, testing to see how tender it was. It was sore, but not bad. Was he trying to clean the wound? Or was he drawn to the dried blood? I wasn't sure. He'd licked my knee too last night.

And today, my knee was completely healed, the bloody scrape gone.

I wanted to tell him, but I couldn't seem to get my brain to communicate with my tongue. He was so warm. Heat rolled off him. Weren't reptiles cold blooded? How did he shift back? Did it hurt?

I had so many questions, but all I could manage to get my mouth to say was a few garbled syllables. "Kroktl."

20

KROKTL

The grid stretched out in my mind like a vast universe of twinkling stars. Only these stars were connected by super-fast neural pathways. Masking my presence on the grid was easy. Making contact with one of the glowing stars—which represented another squad—without anyone else knowing was the difficult part.

Dyni squads were so psychically connected on the grid that it was nearly impossible to distinguish an individual from the rest of their squad. What one member knew, we all knew.

And there was a fucking traitor on my squad.

Shutting down our individual access to the grid allowed us to move separately without sharing our location or plans with Axxol. But that also meant we were unable to track each other or coordinate our movements. We were bred to function as a complete and cohesive team, communicating our plans effortlessly without thought. Denying ourselves access to the grid had taken away one of our greatest advantages, especially in the field, stranded on an inhospitable planet.

Despite the expansive grid that flowed in all directions

across the multiverse, I would normally have been able to pinpoint my squad's twinkling star with ease. Since we were all shut down, I had to improvise.

Sadly, it was like etching a message into the side of a deep-space beacon and casting it adrift through a black hole, hoping it would end up flashing the message to the right person, who was also looking in the right direction, at the exact perfect time, and would bother to read the cryptic scribbles. Despite the squad being broken apart, I had utmost faith in our abilities. We were the fucking best. We'd been sent here on a risky mission for that reason.

And the fucking best comms specialist would be scanning this entire planet for such a message. Knowing Rizan, he'd been calculating our estimated locations this whole time and then narrowing his search down to those projected areas. He wouldn't have to scan the entire planet. He'd already have the probabilities figured out where each of us were hiding.

I connected to the grid for one brief second to flash an SOS. Then I immediately disconnected. Hopefully he'd see the call. He'd be smart enough to locate Snryx and bring him along for the ride.

Most likely, he'd have Lohr too. Three raw dyni males that might all be in rut. I had to assume that they were in heat too, because a squad usually went through the cycle together. A squad did everything together. I was handicapped by being alone on this fucking planet.

But what would my human mate think of an entire squad of dyni in sexual overdrive?

Would she even consider another male? Let alone three more. And if so, how did I feel about that?

My squad? I could immediately picture it. All of us protecting her, fully dedicated to her every wish and desire. They were more than my brothers. They were as much a part of me as she was now, and I'd destroy everything in the universe to protect her. Adding her to our squad would complete us in a way that I'd never dared hope. But if she wasn't interested…

I'd have to hold them off. I wouldn't allow them to traumatize her in any way.

Without a doubt, I could hold my own against them, even three to one. I was bigger now, pumped full of hormones from a successful mating. As long as Axxol wasn't listening on the grid, I'd come out on top. If our BGR came to investigate, I was dead. He'd fucking slaughter me in a heartbeat, and probably the other three as well. I had to hope that he'd feel a heat response for Natalie too and spare her life.

Breathing in her scent, I licked the swollen spot on her head, trying to ease her pain. Would she accept another dynos as easily as she'd accepted me? My ego rejected that thought instantly, but logically, I found the scientific question interesting. Which had come first, biologically speaking? If I hadn't been in heat when I found her, would she have been attracted to me? Was it my scent and hormones that had lured her in despite her fear?

A human mate. Improbable. Impossible.

Priceless.

And she's fucking mine.

21

NATALIE

I woke with a jolt. Something pressed over my mouth. Claws dug into my cheek, pricking but not hurting. Red eyes flashing a warning. Now that I was awake, Kroktl tucked me down into a slight crack in a cliff. Hiding me.

Fuuuuuck. What was wrong? I had to bite my lip to keep from asking him out loud. Someone must be coming for him to hide me. Someone not human. Humans he'd just go eat. Instead, he bumped his chin against the top of my head, silently telling me to stay down as he crouched over me.

This time, I had absolutely no urge to flee.

I couldn't see much at all. It was dark, so I must have been out a few hours. The jungle was eerily silent, just like the night I'd stumbled across his path. Something was out there. Something that even panthers and jaguars feared.

Something that worried Kroktl enough that he practically sat on my back and head. Though I could see a sliver of beach. I didn't hear anything but something blurred by. Close. Only a shadow, I thought, until I heard the snap of Kroktl's teeth. He lunged out, crazy fast, but then settled back over the top of me.

My heart pounded, which didn't help my head at all. It felt like an ice pick drilled into my left temple. My stomach heaved with the pain. It was all I could do to swallow down the bile threatening to boil up out of my throat.

Something thudded against Kroktl. A heaviness that pressed his belly down against my hiding place, blocking the sliver of beach. For a moment, I couldn't breathe, smashed between his monster and the rock. But then he was gone.

Literally gone. I couldn't see him anywhere. Not on the beach. I strained to hear him. See something against the darkness. Terror clutched my heart, urging me to pop up my head and look for him. Leap to my feet. Run.

No. Don't run. Never, ever run.

Something screeched, a high, loud, shrill sound that made me clamp my hands over my ears. I whimpered softly, biting my lip. That sound was nails-on-chalkboard horrible. I didn't think Kroktl had made that screech, but I couldn't be sure.

A huge dark shape landed a few feet away, so heavy that I felt the earth rumble beneath me. I wasn't sure what it was at first, but then he stretched up to his full, impressive height. Kroktl threw his head back and let out a deafening roar that made me whimper again. A warning to whatever had pulled him off me.

What the fuck was big enough to pick him up? My teeth chattered at the thought. His squad. He'd mentioned that he might call them for help. If they were his friends... why were they attacking?

I wished that I could talk to him and ask what the fuck was going on.

His tail slithered over the rocks and touched my cheek. Then pressed on my head, pushing me down. Checking to be sure I was still there, still alright, and then hiding me, even when he was in the middle of a fight. His scent changed, but I couldn't put my finger on it. More feral, maybe? Dark fluid leaked from his temples again. I didn't remember the fluid when he'd carried me out of camp, but I hadn't been paying attention.

A huge, dark shape swept down silently from the sky. Talons extended. A pointed beak that looked as sharp as a spear and just as long. Kroktl whirled, his tail whipping around to strike at the creature in the sky, but it still tore scratches down his back.

Wounds. He was hurt. Blood. That was the smell, the difference in his scent.

Bullets hadn't hurt him. That told me exactly what kind of danger we were in.

Another dynos. It had to be. I just hadn't expected fucking *wings*.

He'd said the medic was spiny something or other. So this flying monster wasn't him.

There. Another dark shape shot up out of the water like a crocodile. It had a long, toothy snout that snapped at Kroktl. A fan of spikes ran along the long, snake-like neck, down its back all the way to its tail. Which it used as a club, tearing into his flank.

Seemingly unbothered by the wounds, Kroktl kicked out one massive leg, claws glistening as he tore a hunk out of the spiny monster's side. The winged one circled overhead, too high for him to reach. Its wingspan made it look like an airplane. Maybe not a commercial jet but pretty damned big.

Something dripped on my head. A sticky glob ran down my forehead, distracting me from the fight. I swiped the stuff away, inwardly shuddering at its snotty texture. Another plop on my nape. Hot, gooey, viscous liquid that slithered down my skin.

Panicked, I hunched down, afraid to look. But more

heavy plops of liquid goo hit my back. It was right there. Standing over me.

I flopped around in a quick roll, hands up, wrists crossed to protect my face.

In the dark, I couldn't see much. Huge, clawed feet braced on either side of the crack where Kroktl had hidden me. A long, forked tongue flicked over my wrists. Past my hands. Tasting me. While more sticky goo dripped from its gaping maw.

Twisting my head as far away as possible, I let out a high-pitched yet oddly hushed scream.

If that tongue touched my face…

I was going to fucking lose my mind.

"Kroktl!"

Thank you for reading Monstrous Heat! I'm hard at work on Monstrous Hunger to continue Natalie's introduction to her Dynosauros squad.

BOOKS BY JOELY SUE BURKHART

Dynosauros
MONSTROUS HEAT
MONSTROUS HUNGER
MONSTROUS HUNT

Their Vampire Queen
Shara Isador
QUEEN TAKES KNIGHTS
QUEEN TAKES KING
QUEEN TAKES QUEEN
QUEEN TAKES ROOK
QUEEN TAKES CHECKMATE
QUEEN TAKES TRIUNE
QUEEN TAKES MORE

HOUSE ISADOR BOXED SET
(Knights – Triune)

Gwen Camelot

QUEEN TAKES CAMELOT

Mayte Zaniyah
QUEEN TAKES JAGUARS

Helayna Ironheart
QUEEN TAKES DARKNESS 1
QUEEN TAKES DARKNESS 2
QUEEN TAKES DARKNESS 3

Karmen Sunna
QUEEN TAKES SUNFIRES 1
QUEEN TAKES SUNFIRES 2
QUEEN TAKES SUNFIRES 3

Xochitl Zaniyah
PRINCESS TAKES ACADEMY 1
PRINCESS TAKES ACADEMY 2
PRINCESS TAKES ACADEMY 3

Belladonna Titanes
QUEEN TAKES VENOM (prequel)
QUEEN TAKES VENOM 1
QUEEN TAKES VENOM 2
QUEEN TAKES VENOM 3

Their Vampire Queen Returns
COMING SOON

Her Irish Treasures Trilogy
SHAMROCKED

LEPRECHAUNED
EVIL EYED

Carnal Heat: A Dark Monster Reverse Harem Romance
CARNAL HEAT

The Shanhasson Trilogy
THE BROKEN QUEEN OF SHANHASSON (free prequel)
THE ROSE OF SHANHASSON
THE ROAD TO SHANHASSON
RETURN TO SHANHASSON

THE COMPLETE SHANHASSON TRILOGY

Dragon Cursed
FREE MY DRAGON
SAVE MY DRAGON

A Jane Austen Space Opera
LADY WYRE'S REGRET (free prequel)
LADY DOCTOR WYRE
LORD REGRET'S PRICE

HER GRACE'S STABLE

The Connaghers
LETTERS TO AN ENGLISH PROFESSOR **(free prequel)**
DEAR SIR, I'M YOURS

HURT ME SO GOOD
YOURS TO TAKE
NEVER LET YOU DOWN
MINE TO BREAK

THE CONNAGHERS BOXED SET

Billionaires in Bondage
THE BILLIONAIRE SUBMISSIVE
THE BILLIONAIRE'S INK MISTRESS
THE BILLIONAIRE'S CHRISTMAS BARGAIN

Zombie Category Romance
THE ZOMBIE BILLIONAIRE'S VIRGIN WITCH

The Wellspring Chronicles
NIGHTGAZER

Other Free Reads
THEIR TYGRESS
THE VICIOUS

Joely Sue Burkhart writing as Sharan Daire

My Over The Top Possessive Alpha Harem
BROKE DOWN
KNOCKED UP
FOUR MEN & A BABY

BROKE DOWN TRILOGY

BLIZZARD BOUND

Made in the USA
Monee, IL
16 April 2023